BY KAREN JENNINGS

Crooked Seeds

An Island

Upturned Earth

Finding Soutbek

CROOKED SEEDS

Crooked Seeds

KAREN JENNINGS

HOGARTH

LONDON NEW YORK

Copyright © 2024 by Karen Jennings

All rights reserved.

Published in the United States by Hogarth, an imprint of Random House, a division of Penguin Random House LLC, New York.

HOGARTH is a trademark of the Random House Group Limited, and the H colophon is a trademark of Penguin Random House LLC.

Grateful acknowledgment is make to Georges Borchardt, Inc. on behalf of the Estate of John Ashbery for permission to reprint four lines from "Soonest Mended" from *The Double Dream of Spring* by John Ashbery, copyright © 1966, 1967, 1968, 1969, 1970, 1997, 2008 by John Ashbery. Reprinted by permission of Georges Borchardt, Inc. on behalf of the author's estate. All rights reserved.

LIBRARY OF CONGRESS CATALOGING-IN-PUBLICATION DATA
NAMES: Jennings, Karen, 1982– author.
TITLE: Crooked seeds / Karen Jennings.
DESCRIPTION: First Edition. | London; New York: Hogarth, [2024]
IDENTIFIERS: LCCN 2023014637 (print) | LCCN 2023014638 (ebook) |
ISBN 9780593597125 (Hardback) | ISBN 9780593597132 (Ebook)
SUBJECTS: LCGFT: Detective and mystery fiction. | Novels.
CLASSIFICATION: LCC PR9369.4.J48 C76 2024 (print) |
LCC PR9369.4.J48 (ebook) | DDC 823/.92—dc23/eng/20230327
LC record available at https://lccn.loc.gov/2023014637
LC ebook record available at https://lccn.loc.gov/2023014638

Printed in Canada on acid-free paper

randomhousebooks.com

9 8 7 6 5 4 3 2 1

FIRST EDITION

Book design by Casey Hampton

For Robert

For this is action, this not being sure, this careless

Preparing, sowing the seeds crooked in the furrow,

Making ready to forget, and always coming back

To the mooring of starting out, that day so long ago.

—From "Soonest Mended" by John Ashbery

PART ONE

PART ONE

Deidre

She woke with the thirst already upon her, still in her clothes, cold from having slept on top of the covers. Two days, three, since she had last changed; the smell of her overcast with sweat, fried food, cigarettes. Underwear's stink strong enough that it reached her even before she moved to squat over an old plastic mixing bowl that lived beside the bed. She steadied her weight on the bed frame with one hand, the other holding on to the seat of a wooden chair that creaked as she lowered herself. She didn't have to put the light on, knew by the burn and smell that the urine was dark, dark as cough syrup, as sickness.

There was no toilet paper, so she rose without wiping, pulling the underwear back into place, feeling it dampen a little. Usually she would reach across, open the window, empty the bowl over the rockery that lined that part of the building's wall, but there had been complaints, a warning. Instead, she took a T-shirt that was lying on the floor and covered the mouth of the bowl with it, before sitting down on the chair. In sleep, the plate of her top front teeth had come loose, protruding a little over her lips. Impossible with her dry mouth to push it back into place. She pulled, snagging it on cracked skin, causing her to switch on the lamp, to feel for blood with her fingertips. None. Then put the teeth on the bedside table next to a mug from which the tea had long since evaporated.

She shifted her leg, lazy to reach for crutches where she had dropped them the night before. It was no distance from the chair to the place described as a kitchen, with its bar fridge, sink, counter, and microwave. She took hold of the chairback, the chest of drawers, the TV stand, the various items that she had refused to give up and which she had crammed into this room, making her way slowly across to the fridge. She did not bother to move onwards to the sink, knowing that the taps would be empty. The microwave clock read 05:18. Forty minutes before the water truck came. Nothing until then.

Inside the fridge was a packet of discolored Vienna sausages, opened a week ago; half a tub of margarine; a jar of gherkins. She unscrewed the lid of the jar, drank down the brine, closing her mouth against its solids, then reached for a Vienna to blunt the sting, its puckered ends like plastic. She spat out what couldn't be chewed, ate two more, spat again, then drew her forearm across her mouth, seeing afterward the smear of grit and slime, and flakes of hideous pink.

The morning's chill reached her as she approached the front entrance of the building. She thought about going back for a jacket, but went on, greeting the security guard as he came across from his hut to open the door for her. "Hey, Winston, here we go again."

"That's right, that's it. Same again."

She could see the queue from where they stood. It ran three blocks deep, extended around the corner. Two armed guards patrolled the outer edges, one more stood near the water truck and collection point. Beyond the truck, a traffic officer had parked his car, the lights flashing hotly in the morning gloom. He had put out cones, was directing the few vehicles that passed by. Passengers and drivers looked out at the queue, at the people with their array of containers, in dressing gowns and slippers, wearing jackets and coats over their work clothes and school uniforms, a few wrapped in blankets against the cold. Someone was listening to the news on a cellphone, elsewhere music was playing. Most were using earphones though, intent on something beyond this slow, shifting wait. Few were interested in conversation.

"How's it looking today?" she said.

"Nothing special. Same as always. I didn't see you yesterday, you okay?"

"Ja, just wasn't in the mood for all this shit."

He nodded. "Ja, I know what you mean."

She eyed the queue, saw a woman with a teenage daughter, the girl's arms crossed, the mother's too. They wore headscarves and long skirts. Behind them stood a man with his son and daughter. The man tapped his foot, leaned forward, and said something to the scarved woman. She shook her head, then took out her phone and showed him something on it, the light from the screen highlighting the darkness beneath her eyes. The man frowned, rubbed hard at his jaw in irritation.

Deidre had already taken a few steps toward the queue, but she came back now, said to Winston, "Give us a ciggy, hey? I'll get you back later."

"When's later? I'm still waiting from last week and last month. Eish man, I'm still waiting from last year." But he took one from his pocket, lit it, handed it across.

She coughed wetly as she inhaled, then spat the wet out. "Ag, man, don't be like that. One day I'm going to bring you a whole pack, okay? Like a whole pack, and not just any kind. It'll be the good kind, you'll see."

"Ja, I'm waiting . . ."

She blew him a kiss, adjusted the backpack that she wore slung over one shoulder—an old thing from her daughter's high school years, tearing a little at the seams. "Bye, darling, let me get this over and done with."

A dull sunrise held back beyond the streetlamps and she crutched toward it, into the road, ignoring the cone markers so that cars had to stop for her, three in a row. She kept her eyes on the water truck, did not acknowledge the cars, did not look at the queue. She went deliberately slowly, pausing every few steps to remove the cigarette from her mouth, to exhale, inhale again. Before leaving her room she had brushed her hair; applied makeup over the previous day's smudges; sprayed her armpits, crotch, and hair; licked toothpaste from her finger; reinserted her plate. She wore now a skirt that came to mid-thigh, showing the blanched scar at her stump, and a T-shirt of cheap black lace that revealed a purple bra, her breasts high and hard.

She tossed the cigarette end at the gutter, moved toward the trestle table at the front of the queue, where two water monitors were taking turns to fill containers from a tap in the truck's side.

"Hey, lady," someone called, "there's a line here, you know. Go to the back!"

She made no sign that she had heard, beckoned instead to the armed guard. "A little help, please."

"Sure, ma'am." He was young, his uniform still new,

shoes stiff and bright, so that his steps toward her were wide-legged, heavy.

"Oh darling," she smiled and shifted the backpack from her shoulder, "just call me Deidre."

He returned the smile, removed an empty three-liter Coke bottle from her backpack. "Well, Deidre, can I have your ID, please?"

She put her hand in her pocket, slowly pulling the skirt downwards to reveal part of her belly, and took out her card. "Here you go, darling, but don't look at it. The photo's so bad."

"Oh, come on, you look great! Really, it's a good picture, I'm telling you." Then, "Hold on a sec. I'll be right back with your water, okay?"

"Sure, sure, take your time."

But almost at once she began tapping her fingers on the crutch handles, her throat dry and wanting. She glanced across at the queue, hoping to catch an eye, to ask if someone had a cigarette, but no one looked at her. Nothing else to see in the dawn other than rooftops starting to appear slowly, a series of them, going back and back into the gray light, each straddling something dark and stillborn—the empty rooms of empty homes. So many people had left. Yet even in the ones that were inhabited, there was only darkness. Everyone was here now, in this queue. There was no other life.

At her foot a small stream of water was starting to pool. Deidre moved, let the water pass, looking back up along its damp path to the truck, where one of the monitors was picking up a container that had fallen. Both monitors were wet across their bellies and thighs, both frowning as they went between the trestle table and the tap. The woman was filling Deidre's bottle now, handing it back to the guard, then turned to the next in line, a young man dressed in a suit and tie. He had an ID in each hand, held them out to the woman, began to speak.

Behind Deidre a car drove slowly past, its undercarriage low, scraping across a speed bump. People winced at the sound, glanced with caution at the driver and his passengers, with their arms slung casually from the windows, skin blue with homemade tattoos. Deidre glared at them, wanted to call out and ask what they were looking at, but she knew what they were and what they could do. She glanced away, counted the guards, turned to look at Winston, checked if he had a gun, knowing that he didn't. Yet even if he had, even then it would have made no difference. So, she waited, watched the car with lowered eyes, seeing it begin to speed up, drive on.

When she turned back toward the truck, the man at the front of the queue had raised his voice. "You see, she's sick. She can't come." Then, to a question, "Yes, my mother, she's my mother."

But, "No, that's not true. He's lying!" called a woman, stepping out from the queue. "He's a liar. He's lying to you. His mother died two weeks ago. I was at her funeral, for God's sake. I'm telling you, he's lying."

The man shook his head. "I'm sorry, you're mistaken, lady, my mother's at home, she's not dead, she's just sick. You're mistaken." Then to the monitor, "I can call her; look, I'll video-call her, okay?"

The woman was crying now. "No, you mustn't believe him. He's lying. I knew her and she's dead. This isn't right. What you're doing isn't right. You're lying. She's dead."

The young guard had Deidre's water in his hand, but he walked over to the woman, held his arm out toward the queue. "I have to ask you to get back in line, ma'am. Leave this to us, we'll sort it out. Let's just all try to be calm, please."

"But he's lying. I'm telling you." Still, she allowed herself to be guided back to where her boy stood. He clutched at her legs and began to wail as she said, "I can't do this anymore, I can't do it. Better to be dead, I'd rather be dead."

Around her people shuffled uneasily, moving away so that the boy and woman stood alone, each gulping and desperate while the guard pointed at them. "Now, listen, you'll have to be quiet, okay? I told you, we'll sort this out. You can't be like this, okay?"

Deidre waited, grew tired. "Hey," she called, "can I have my water now?"

He turned around, frowning, but smiled when he saw her, coming across with the bottle. "Sorry you had to see that," he said, raising his eyebrows and shaking his head. "It gets ugly like this sometimes, you know."

"Ja, people are shit."

He handed back her ID. "You know, you really do look great, like I'd never guess your age. You're like really sexy."

She put her hand on his forearm. "Well, you're making my day, darling. A strong handsome thing like you. I could eat you up."

The guard blushed, eyed her bra, her stomach. "Well, let me carry this back for you; it's not a problem."

There was the temptation to say yes, to invite him to her room. But she remembered the bowl of piss, the smell of her underwear. "Ah, thanks, darling, I can manage by myself. You've got too much going on here today."

"Well, ja, it's kind of crazy." He helped her put the bottle into the backpack and placed it on her shoulders. "But next time, okay?"

"Ja, next time, definitely."

She boiled some of the water, pouring it into an empty five-liter ice cream container taken from the building's recycling area. The plastic softened under the heat, the container bending a little away from her grasp, so that she thought it might slip or tear and the water be lost. Instead, she dragged it across the counter, adding cold water from the Coke bottle to temper the heat, then removed her clothes, leaving them on the counter beside it. She pulled a tall stool toward her, sat down, and unlaced her shoe, sighing at the effort to come.

From a drawer she took a dishcloth and dipped it in the container. The water was still hot, burned her fingers, but was good on her skin, leaving her with chills as she rubbed herself damp. She had forgotten about soap and stretched across for a sticky bottle of green dishwashing liquid beside the sink. She poured some on the cloth, began to scrub. The liquid foamed under her arms, made the air hard with the scent of something meant to be lemon. Long hairs grew in her armpits, on her leg too, but it was too far to the bathroom, too far when she hadn't entered it in months and didn't know whether she had a razor or not.

When she was done, she rang the cloth out grayly, then plunged it in once more, shivering at the heat, her back cold and goose-bumped. She went over her body again, and another time, until she had had enough. Then she lowered her head as best she could into the container. Afterward she poured dishwashing liquid onto the palm of one hand and worked it through the wet and dry of her hair while sitting. She rinsed once, though the water was largely suds now and they remained heavy in her hair. She pulled the strands together at the side of her neck, pressed water back into the container.

Finally, she took her bra and panty from the pile of clothes, pushed them into the ice cream container a few times, releasing a fishy smell that lingered despite the addition of dishwashing liquid. After a while she brought the panty up to her nose, sniffed the crotch. Clean enough. She squeezed out the excess water, shook loose the suds, hung the underwear over the kitchen tap.

The floor was wet, soapy, and she made her way to the bed with care, water cooling as it ran down her neck and back. She climbed in under the covers, smelled the earthiness of them, easily a year since they had been washed, the pillow worst of all, made still worse by her wet hair. She pulled the duvet up to her chin, turning her head a little to get away from the smell of it. As she dried, her skin tightened, began to itch. She reached down, scratched her calf, both thighs. Her scalp, too, seemed to be crawling. She closed her eyes against the feeling, let her skin creep until she'd willed it to stop. In the kitchen, the sound of her underwear dripping into the basin, and beyond it the faint noises of the queue. Within, a throat sick with need.

She had stood up again, had dressed, and was waiting with her door open. There were footsteps; a child running. She called out as he passed her, "Hey, you forgotten me?"

The boy stopped, came back a little way, his eyes fixed on her stump.

"Where you going in such a hurry, hey?"

"We're going on a outing and we don't have to wear our uniform."

"That's nice." She couldn't remember his name. "Where they taking you?"

"This place that used to be like a wetland and my teacher says a hippo used to live there and they had lots of birds and stuff, but now it's like all endangered."

"Ja, I remember that hippo. It's dead now."

"How'd it die?"

"From eating too many children."

He made a face. "I'm not stupid."

"So, be clever and think what you want, but don't come crying to me when you meet a hippo one day and it bites off your leg and you look like me."

"That's not how you lost your leg."

"Isn't it?" Then, "Listen, is your mom home?"

"Uh-huh, she's changing Roxy."

"Okay, I'll just pop over. You go on, and watch out for those hippos."

He was already running, his backpack clapping against him.

She walked one door up, her crutches muffled on the worn blue carpet. There were large stains, brown-haloed cigarette burns, gaps where the carpet had been torn up and not replaced. The door was ajar and she pushed it open with a crutch. "Hello, hello, it's only me."

Miriam stood at the counter, lifting Roxy's legs with one hand, sliding a nappy underneath with the other. The basin held used wet wipes, paper plates, and a plastic knife. Miriam didn't look up, said, "Oh, hi." Then, when she'd finished with the nappy, "That's done." She picked up the baby and leaned against the counter. There were no chairs, the room full with a double bed, crib, and a large TV mounted on the wall. "So, how're you?"

"Ja, you know, fine. And you?"

"Tired."

"Where's Alistair? I thought you said he was off this week?"

"Nah, a water truck's been hijacked, so he had to fly up to P.E. yesterday because they've got a spare up there and now he has to drive it down."

"Jesus."

"Ja, he says he has an armed escort, but what does that actually mean? Some child that failed high school now has a rifle? How does that help? Anyway, I'm making him send me a message every hour so I know he's okay."

Roxy began to whine and Miriam hushed her, holding her to her chest.

"Listen," said Deidre, "I was wondering . . ."

Miriam rolled her eyes. "Here we go."

"No, it's just, can you clean my place quickly? Just a mop. The floor's already wet, so it's pretty much already done. It'll be two minutes max. And listen, listen, you can even have some tea—I picked up my water this morning and there's half of it still left."

"Ah, do it yourself, man. I know you can, I've seen you do it."

"Come on, I don't have a mop; that last one broke. And it's just quicker if you do it. Two minutes, a minute. Come on, help me out. Look at me, I'm a fucking cripple."

"Oh Jesus, Deidre, you're terrible."

The baby continued to fuss and Deidre put out a finger to stroke her hand. "Such a cutie, such a sweet little cutie."

Miriam sighed. "You'll have to watch her while I'm doing it, okay?"

"Sure, no problem."

She moved across to the unmade bed and sat down, setting aside her crutches and holding out her arms for the baby.

"Three minutes, that's it. That's all the time I have. I need to get things sorted here for that inspector."

"It's today?"

"Uh-huh. Maybe if he sees the shithole they expect a family of four to live in, then he'll get us moved. I mean, you can't expect children to live in a single room in a fucking retirement village. Even if it is supposed to be temporary."

"Well, don't get your hopes up, you know. It's all promises-promises and nothing ever comes from it. I mean, you know that, you know it already. Like, they took our houses for fuck's sake, they took them and they promised to pay us, but where's the money and where are we? That's what I want to fucking know."

Miriam clicked her tongue. "I don't have time for this today. Just sit there with Roxy and I'll be back."

She grabbed a mop, was getting a bottle of floor cleaner from under the sink when Deidre said, "Oh, listen, if you want that cup of tea, you'll have to take your own tea bag. I don't have any."

"For fuck's sake, Deidre. You really are something else."

Deidre bounced the baby, holding her under the armpits, speaking nonsense words into her face. Roxy looked back, burbling as she tried to push a fist into her mouth. There were tiny red bumps across her cheeks and a sour smell that seemed to come from her neck and the sodden front of her onesie.

"You're a dirty little thing, aren't you?"

Still, she bent forward, sniffed the dark fluff of her head, then gave her a finger to play with, let her put it in her mouth and gum it softly. There had been moments like this before in her life. Moments of tenderness, of love. A long time ago, more than thirty years since she had held her daughter as a baby. A living thing among them after they had existed on char and rubble for so long.

Deidre's father had been retrenched by then, had been told to make way for those who had previously been over-looked under the old conventions. He'd said no word against it, already having spent more time than permitted on leave. Hours at her mother's bedside, hours at her own. Hours of waiting as piece by piece they cut away bone and muscle, leaving her with her deformities.

She used to lie awake in that wide, aging ward with its high ceilings and the row of beds on either side that seemed to extend endlessly away from her, each one of them inhabited by a version of herself, each version more whole the further away it lay. And the last one, her complete self, little more than an apparition that vanished with each blinking. There were no radios in that ward, no televisions. Only her father's voice, sitting beside her, reading from a newspaper, and she wondered which version of him this was and how many repetitions of him there were that she couldn't see.

He read to her about the approaching Rugby World

Cup final between the Springboks and the All Blacks, told her what it meant to him, to everybody. It was like being allowed to come out of confinement, he said. Like being given permission to be something again and to move in the world without shame. He put his hand on hers, asked her to look at him and she did, her eyes burning as she tried to hear clearly, to follow his lips through her medication. He was asking would she mind if the next day he didn't come, if just this one time he went instead to a bar and watched the game with friends. Would it be okay? She had nodded, said, "I hope we win."

Yet when the victory had come, she had not known what it was. Afterward they explained that it had been fireworks, but on that day she saw only a great roaring flame that rose and fell in multicolor, casting a blaze into the room along the rows of apparitions that set them in shimmering motion. There was heat around her, heat and shimmering life, all of it on the point of being interrupted, torn jagged by the blaze. She called out to them, threw herself from the bed, falling to a crawl and moving toward her distant self. But she was dragged up, held down, and injected, so that the room became a dull bewilderment.

Her father returned to her bedside. He pointed out headlines and pictures in the newspapers. This was the one who scored the winning drop goal; this the one it took three men to tackle. This man, here, and his wife had taken down their fence and let the whole neighborhood watch on a sheet in their garden. And here, look here, a black boy and a white boy were both wearing Springbok jerseys, their arms around one another. "Doesn't it make a tear come to your eyes? Can't you feel this thing, like a promise?" he'd said.

He had yogurt for her and spooned it into her mouth, though she could have done it herself. Later, he peeled a naartjie for them to share, crushing the skin "for the nice smell," but really it was to cover the stink of her. That same stink that followed her for years afterward, just like the itches and shudders that caused her even now to scratch at a thing that had long since been removed.

There was no queue, the truck and cones gone a while since. Only, in places, there lingered dull marks from where water had leaked earlier. The sky was dull too, dull and cold, with a ruffle of clouds over the mountain that might at one time have promised rain. But in recent years everything that had once been certain had become indecipherable.

She had taken a denim jacket before leaving her room, and she put it on now outside the security hut, hoping Winston would come back soon from wherever he'd stepped out to so that she could bum another cigarette. She waited, buttoned the jacket. Her throat ached. She reached into a small bag slung over her chest and brought out her phone. Two missed calls from a withheld number; they'd been coming steadily for a couple of days, never leaving a voicemail. She clicked her tongue, deleted the notifications, looked at the time. 10:38.

Across the road a man in blue workers' overalls scrubbed at graffiti on the wall of the high school. FUCK CORRUPTION WHERES OUR WATER? Deidre looked at her phone again, put it away, began to crutch toward the man, thinking he might have a cigarette. But a woman came out of the school entrance and stopped him in his labor, and Deidre paused, still on her side of the road. They spoke softly, the conversation ending abruptly: "No, there's just no budget for paint." The woman glanced across at Deidre, looked at her stump, looked away again, went back inside. The man returned to his scrubbing. She could feel the rasping of it all around her, a tunnel of smarting sound, all bristles and ringing, bright in her ears, so that she had to turn away, shake her head, tilt the noise out of herself.

Irritated, she stepped into the road, crossing diagonally away from him. She stopped at the far corner of the block, outside a blue building with two thick pillars holding up an overhang above the stoep. There was a triangular gable with the raised numbers 1911 painted white. She did not enter, waited at the bottom of three steps that were too steep for her to climb easily and for which she was not in the mood.

"Hussain!" she called. "Hey, Hussain!"

A bearded man in a kufi came out, cleaning his spectacles on a beige fleece. "Ah, Deidre, good morning." He replaced the spectacles, blinking a little. "How are you today?"

"Ag, you know how it is. Everything's shit and then we die."

He pulled his mouth tight, brought his hands together at his waist. "What can I do for you?"

She dug around in her bag, pulled out a few silver coins. "Pack of Stuyvesant."

He looked at her hand. "Please, Deidre, you know that isn't enough. You know how much it costs."

"Ah, come on. How much money do I spend here? Give me a break just this once, okay?"

"You can't say that. You know it isn't just this once. It's every time now. I have my bills and my family and I can't always be giving away things for free, do you understand? You want my advice, get a job."

"Oh, a job? That's great advice, thank you. Tell me, who's hiring fifty-three-year-old cripples that didn't finish high school? Can you tell me, because I really want to know."

He came down the steps, took the coins from her. "This is enough for four singles. Do you want or not?"

"So, bring them. I can't stay here all day wasting my time. I have somewhere I need to be."

He went back inside. There were no lights on despite the clouded sky, and she could not make out anything from where she stood, though she knew well enough what it looked like: a glass counter with its display of loose sweets, flaking samosas, toiletries, packets of salt-and-vinegar chips. Behind the counter, fridges crammed with cheap cool drinks, milk close to its expiration date, and pies in sealed wax paper bags that you could ask to be taken to the back and microwaved. Next to the fridges were shelves of water in bottles of different sizes, from two hundred milliliters to five liters, and a large sign, official, that said the shop owner had permission to carry a firearm.

Hussain came back, held out six singles. She took them, put them in her purse. "Take this," he said, giving her a strawberry-flavored drinking yogurt. "You're too thin. You need to take care of yourself." He was already up the stairs again, waving his hand behind his back to indicate that she shouldn't reply.

She stood a moment, lit a cigarette, checked her phone—10:49—then walked on, passing the park, the dry sorrow of it. A few pigeons picked at nothings on the cracked tar. There'd been grass here at one time, and sometimes she and her dad had stopped with Monica to play. Friday afternoons she had art class in a garage-studio nearby with an old friend of Deidre's mother. The classes were free to Monica, the woman saying, "It's a shame, all that your family's suffered. A real shame." She looked at Deidre's crutches. "This new South Africa, hey? It's put more than just your mother into a depression, and you can't blame people for feeling that way."

It had never been much, the park. Not large enough for soccer games or anything like that, but nice in its way. Nice enough to stop the car and let Monica have a go on the swings while her little clay bowl or painting dried on the backseat. But now the climbing frame was chipped away to brown, had names and words scratched into it, half the bars

missing. It would have been better to dismantle it alto-
gether, along with the seesaw and the top of the merry-go-
round. Only the bases of these remained cemented in place
and, at the far end of the park, the rusted scaffold with its
chains that had once held swings made of old tires. Children never played here anymore. The place reeked of piss,
of shit too, and had been taken over by three bergies and
their dogs. They lived in homes made from discarded sheets
of fiberglass and other scraps, wandering the streets in turn,
searching out glass bottles and tin cans to take to the recycling depot over the bridge in exchange for a little money.
But most of the day they spent in the nearby bar's parking
lot, guiding drivers into empty bays and watching the cars
from old plastic crates under a large tree.

Two of them were in the park now, sitting in a patch of
sun, frowning upward, letting it warm their faces. But they
rose when they saw Deidre passing, and came across to the
place in the fence where there had once been a gate. Behind
them a black-and-white short-legged mongrel stretched
and followed, its tail wagging.

"Mornings," Deidre said, then, "Hi, Boontjie, hi," bending forward to scratch his head and let him lick her hand.
"Where's Queenie?"

"Ag," said Sussie, "you know that dog is in love with
Rodney. You can't stop her following him when he goes
out."

Boontjie rolled over, was showing his belly. "Jirre,

you're getting fat. You need to go out walking with Queenie, you fatty."

Sussie laughed. "Ja, it's that lady from the SPCA, she's always bringing stuff for them. Donations from the community, she says, and I say thank you, I'm not going to say no, because I've always said that's how it is, people can find a heart for a dog. Didn't I say that, Bliksem, didn't I say 'a heart for a dog,' but,"she pointed at their home, "what about us, heh?"

"Ja," said Deidre. "That's the way it is."

Sussie nodded, her eyes on Deidre's. "You have anything for us today, my child?"

"Not today. Hussain took my last coins."

"Not even a entjie?"

"This is my last one." But she'd lost the taste for it, said, "Here, I don't want it."

Sussie took it first, passed it to Bliksem, waited for him to pass it back.

"Well . . ." said Deidre, coughing a little.

"Are you going there?" he said, motioning with his head. "It's almost time."

"Ja," she said. "I'm going."

"I'll walk with you."

"I've got nothing, hey. That's all I had." She pointed at the cigarette.

"No, man, it's just a walk with a friend. I'm going there, I have to start my work."

"Okay, I'm just saying, because I know you."

They walked in single file along the narrow pavement, Bliksem calling to her, "You see this weather? You see it?"

"I see it."

"I still got some of my ancestors in me, a little bit of that old Khoisan blood, hey, and it's telling me rain is coming. I'm telling you, it's coming."

She stopped a moment, turned her head. "I don't know, man. I don't trust that blood of yours, it's too weak from all the drink, hey."

He laughed hoarsely. "We'll see, we'll see. A man needs a dop against the cold, you know, just a little dop to keep him alive. It doesn't mean anything, it doesn't change what's true."

They had reached the back of the building, stood just within the parking lot. She could see the side door wasn't open yet and she took out her phone. 10:58. "For fuck's sake, I'll have to go round the front."

"Just wait a minute, my child," he said, taking a seat on his crate under the tree. "They'll open it soon."

But, no, she couldn't wait, her throat uncomfortable in its urgency. She returned her phone to the bag, felt the yogurt there, said, "Listen, I wasn't lying; I don't have anything. But take this, it's good, you'll like it."

"Ah, thank you, my child." He pulled the foil cap off at once, took a sip, his top lip pink from the artificial coloring. "Mmm, nice. Very nice. But try to bring us something tomorrow, heh?"

The building was old, parts of it made of large stones shaped into rough squares. It had been a hotel at one time, then a boardinghouse for derelict men. Now it was the Nine Lives, with a second floor she'd never been to, where you could play on slot machines or have a game of pool, but mostly people did little more than place bets on the day's horse races. The ground floor had a worn mahogany counter, with bottles and glasses stacked along a mirrored wall. The rest of the walls held big-screen televisions, all of them showing races, the same images in motion whichever way you turned.

She was breathless as she rounded the corner, her throat shuddering at the sight of the security gate still closed.

"Hey," she called. "Hey, it's time to open."

Isaac looked up from where he was wiping down tables, said, "Sorry, you'll have to wait a bit. Trains weren't running again . . ."

"How long?"

"Five, ten minutes."

"For fuck's sake."

She went to sit at one of four picnic tables outside, swallowing hard to stop the beating in her throat. She lit a cigarette, checked her phone. 11:03. Another missed call, number withheld, a message from her service provider about some or other deal, and one from Monica: "Ugh morning sickness," followed by three green-faced vomiting emojis. She deleted the others, replied, "sorry darling" to Monica and added a heart, returning the phone to her bag.

She inhaled deeply, narrowed her eyes against the noise of the passing cars, more of them than usual. The traffic light was red and a dreadlocked man beckoned to the motorists, trying to sell *The Big Issue*. There was a face on the cover that she did not recognize, and "Good News at Last." She wondered what the good news was, looked across at the lampposts for the day's headline in case it might be there. There were five poles within her view, each weighed down by party political posters—calls for votes in the upcoming elections, promises of what they would do for the people, the usual bullshit. One of the poles had an advertisement for a comedy show at the Baxter Theatre, another promoted a baby and toddler expo at the Convention Center. There was only one newspaper headline in among all of that: NO RAIN EXPERTS SAY.

She inhaled again, the smoke passing raggedly through

her, and called toward the still-closed security gate as she saw Isaac walking by with a crate of glasses, "Come on, man, how much longer?"

"Five minutes."

The others began to arrive, complaining of the traffic, as though they'd come together, bound to this place at all hours, from all locations.

Ricardo, in his seventies, who always wore the same two hand-knitted pullovers with white-collared shirts. "Mornings, mornings," he said. "People, let me tell you, don't try to go to Muizenberg today, there's protests and the trains are on fire and the traffic's backed up like it's the Second Coming."

"Is it?" said Steven. He was young, early twenties or so, never drank, never gambled. Just sat at his table, watching the races, saying at least once a day that his grandpa had worked at the stables at the Kenilworth Racecourse and it was a pity it had closed down and they only raced in Durban now. Sometimes he made little sounds, dabbed at the sweat on his face and neck with a hand towel he kept with him. He'd been in the army and been sent out to Spine Road, near Khayelitsha, to quash a protest that had gotten violent. That's what Ricardo had told her, but he didn't know more. Only that the boy had developed PTSD and a stutter, had terrible nightmares, so they put him in the state clinic at Stikland for treatment, but in the end there wasn't anything to do for him, and they let him out. He couldn't go back to work though, couldn't even get another job, so he was on disability, like herself. But he could work if he wanted to, if he put his mind to it. He was physically able, there wasn't actually anything wrong with him. That's what Deidre always came back to. There wasn't anything wrong with him. They weren't the same.

Steven spoke again to Ricardo, his body taut with the effort of getting the words out. "They're going to start building the desalination plant at Strandfontein."

Ricardo frowned. "Really? You heard that? I hope it's true, I really do. It's, what, three years now since they forced those people out of that area to build the plant and not a thing's been done yet. Not a damn thing. I never thought, not once, not ever in a million years, that I'd live through a time of forced removals again. I never thought it. Never. But what can we say, governments are all the same in the end, hey? They don't give a damn. If it isn't about race or the drought, it's about something else, and they'll toss people out without a thought."

Marvin, a silver-haired ex-builder, turned to Steven. "Look, there's no way that's possible. The reason they haven't started building yet is because you need water to build—to make the cement. There's no water. There's no money. There's no goddamn cement. It's not gonna happen, let me tell you. Why do you think my business failed? No water, that's why. It's not going to happen. There's no way, okay. Don't be a fucking idiot."

Steven pushed his hands into his pockets, looked at the ground, his cheeks and forehead red.

"Ah, Jesus, Marvin, shut up," said Deidre. "You're a fucking bully. Jesus. Just one morning come in here without fighting and insulting everyone."

"Listen, lady, when you—"

But Isaac was in the doorway, pulling aside the security gate. "Okay, people, we're open. You can come in now."

Ricardo led the way, stopping as he always did at a four-seater in the middle of the room. Isaac brought across the newspaper and Ricardo spread it out, reading with tuts and sighs. From time to time he called out a comment. Steven, sitting at a two-seater beside a thick pillar, nodded in response, wiping the towel across his forehead. Only Marvin headed upstairs, making for the small office where the bets were placed.

Deidre went straight to the bar. "Double rum, Isaac."

"Who's paying?"

"Just put it on my tab."

He shook his head. "No, man, your tab's full. Vadi says nothing more until you've paid."

"Jesus, he acts like I'm a fucking criminal. It's only fucking Red Heart, not like I'm asking for the fancy shit." She took a debit card from her bag, handed it across. "So, give me a Castle draft then, but go easy on the foam, okay. I don't want the foam."

She went to sit at a two-seater beside the window, waited

for Isaac to carry the drink across for her. She watched him coming, his walk slow, the slop of foam over the rim of the glass maddening her, so that "Bring it," she said under her breath, "bring it, bring it." When he arrived, she followed his movements as he pulled a coaster closer and put the glass down in front of her. She placed her hands around the glass at once, feeling the cold of it, the wet, leaning forward until he was gone, then lifting it with trembling hands. She took a small sip at first, swallowing with difficulty, but then something loosened in her throat and she felt able to open wider, to take in more.

Her phone began to ring in her bag. She pulled it out, looked at the screen. Number withheld. She sucked in her cheeks, breathed out, letting it ring once more before answering. "Listen, stop calling here, okay. I'm not interested in your party or any other goddamn party. I'm not voting for anyone, so just stop fucking harassing me."

"Miss van Deventer?"

"Who's this?"

"Good morning, ma'am. This is Detective Constable Xaba from the Diep River branch of the South African Police Service. I have been trying to reach you for several days."

"Oh. What you want?"

"Ma'am, I'm afraid there is a problem at your house—"

"No, no, no, don't start with that. It's not my house anymore. It was taken away. It hasn't been my house for two years."

"Yes, ma'am, I understand that the land was reclaimed, but the problem—"

"That's a nice word, isn't it? Reclaimed. A house my father designed and built with his own hands, with his own hard work, his own money, but the government says no, we're taking it. Oh yes, it's very nice. Talking nice things about the past, the future, about water under the land, and kicking me out."

"Ma'am, please, this has nothing to do with the land reclaim. You will have to take that up with the appropriate department. This is something else. You see, they have begun demolishing and leveling the area now, and some things have been found and we are asking you to come in and identify them."

"What things? What you talking about?"

"Ma'am, if you come in then we can discuss that further."

"Well, I can't. I'm a cripple. I can't get around."

"Yes, ma'am, I see. We can send a car to fetch you." There was a short pause. "At Oak Bend Center, is it?"

"No, I'm not there right now. I'm busy. I'm out."

"Ma'am, I understand, but I'm afraid this is very important. It is a police investigation."

"What you saying? What you investigating?"

"I'd prefer not to discuss it over the phone. Can I send a car for you tomorrow, will that be okay?"

Deidre coughed, cleared her throat. "Ja, okay."

"Excellent, thank you. Detective Sergeant Mabombo will call for you at nine A.M."

Deidre hung up, returned the phone to her bag. When she looked up, the TVs had been switched on, and all around the bar hooves were pounding on grass in vibrant color, racing toward an end they didn't seem able to reach.

Trudy

His jacket over the back of the chair when she opened her eyes. Him standing in front of the window with his arms crossed.

It was the light that woke her, though she hadn't really been asleep. She'd been kept awake all this time by an aching thirst that had left her pressing the call button for hours. She'd heard the food trolley clatter past, smelled the chicken and broccoli. But it had not come to her, had passed by. A blessing really; she could stomach nothing. And there had been voices too, outside her window in the bricked-up area that had at one time been a lawn, but that now baked with heat, trapping it there so that they kept her blinds and curtains drawn against it at all times. A conversation had been taking place, the words lifting up toward her, about a dress and what shoes would match it best. A discussion about straps and heels and colors, and going to look at the mall. Then their voices faded, they were gone, and she had felt an urge to turn to the curtains, whine after them, "Wait for me. I want to come."

All this she had heard in detail, yet somehow he had entered, had opened the curtains, the blind, without her knowing. And for a moment, that first moment of blinking wakefulness, it was the daylight that surprised her more than anything else. Perhaps because she had known him at once, despite the years, despite the receding hairline, the large bald patch at the back of his head. He had on a two-tone shirt, similar to those his father had worn, and belted jeans, a bit slack over the behind. He had always been thin.

"Ross," she said, her mouth too dry to make the sound. She was afraid he hadn't heard her, but he turned at the croak, unfolding his arms as he did.

"You're not sleeping," he said, as though it had not been decades since she'd last seen him. That made her smile, because wasn't that just like him not to make a fuss.

"My boy," she whispered, trying to reach out toward him, but her hand was caught in the folds of the blanket. She struggled, watched as he stepped forward and released it.

"You want some water?" he asked.

She nodded, and he reached for a half-full plastic cup on the bedside table. There was a straw in it. He curled it over, brought it carefully to her lips. Her mouth was so dry that she could hardly manage at first, but then at last it was there. Water, not cool, but wet, wet on her tongue and inside her cheeks. She had not put in her teeth, did not even know where they were, and wondered suddenly if she looked terrible, if she disgusted him, this thing that she had become. But he lifted the straw where it caught on her dry skin and his knuckle touched her without flinching.

She licked her lips, said thank you with a little gasp she had not intended. Then, "Have you been here long?"

"No."

"Did you have far to come?"

"Not really."

"Have you been so close, then, all this time?"

He returned the plastic cup to the bedside table, straightened a piece of paper that was lying there. "Let's not talk about it now, Ma."

"Yes. You're here, that's what I care about. Does Deidre know?"

"Not yet."

"It will be a surprise for her."

He didn't say anything, stood above her, the sunlight behind him so bright that all his features were lost. She closed her eyes against the glare. "Give your mother a kiss, my boy."

He leaned over, smelling, as his father had, of clean clothes, just ironed, of supermarket-bought cologne and cigarette smoke.

"Here you are," she said. "I knew you would come. I knew you wouldn't leave your mother to die and not say goodbye. Not my son." Then, as he put his hand on hers, his fingers coarse, the light seemed to be drawn into him, seemed to be taken up in one long inhalation that pushed him forward. She could see him clearly now, the details of his face. "I didn't realize you'd be so like your father."

It was unexpected. Similar foreheads, cheekbones, ears, and noses. And the way he carried himself was the same, with slumped shoulders, hanging head; men embarrassed by their height. She had not anticipated this, had always imagined, for no good reason, that he would resemble her side of the family. That he would share her brother's features, as they shared a name. But because her brother had not made it to middle age, the man she had imagined her son to take after had been a composite of him and her father, with his oiled hair and slim mustache, jaw round and dimpled. Yet here was her Ross, and he was none of those things, despite blood and genes and names. He was clean shaven, angular, as her husband had been, resembling him so closely that even the voice was an echo.

"But why shouldn't you be like your father?" she said. "It's a surprise, that's all. You spent enough time with him, didn't you, all those weekends fiddling with the lawn mower and the old radios."

"That's right."

Hours of sawing and sanding and painting, and an array of birdhouses in different shapes and colors. Ross climbing up into the three silver trees on the property, hammering the boxes in place, terrifying her where she stood below, a hand over her mouth to keep from screaming, fearful that he might fall and die, and with him all of herself and himself and all the generations that had been and would have been. Her stomach fluttered, she reached out to him, his coarse hand. "The birds didn't even stay in them."

"What's that? What birds?"

"Do you think they could still be there? We'll have to ask Deidre. Remind me to ask her."

There had been more than just the birdhouses though. At twelve he began working on projects by himself, going out to the garage before and after school, spending whole weekends there, with a handwritten sign taped to the door: PRIVATE WORKSHOP. DO NOT ENTER. They had laughed about it, she and Paul, not minding that the Ford Sierra had been forced to stand in the driveway. Starlings splashed their waste on it, leaving parts of the roof and windscreen crusted purple. Deidre complained about that, yes, she complained. Given half a chance she would have spent hours lying in front of the television, watching any old rubbish. "Not in my house," Trudy had said. "That's not how I was raised. A girl must do chores. She must know how to keep herself busy." She drew up a list, allocating tasks to every weekday, more to the weekends, including washing the car.

It was a bone of contention, that list of chores, because Ross had none. But for him it hadn't been necessary. He was always busy, had no time to waste on silly things like that. Not when what he produced was so remarkable. "Just extraordinary," she told the ladies at church. He'd made a desk for his room, a bench for the garden, flower boxes and shelves and small kists with hinges. But then he had grown tired of carpentry, moving on to metal and electrical work. In the evenings, over supper, he asked her to go to the hardware store the next day and pick up little lightbulbs, wires, things she didn't know or understand, all written down for her on a scrap of paper. On Sunday mornings he and his dad went to the flea market at Green Point to scratch through piles of bits and bobs on trestle tables under faded gazebos. He always found something good, something to bring home and work on.

A genius. That's what he was, a real genius. It wasn't just that he was clever or talented. He was something else, something different. That's what she told his principal when called in to discuss Ross's consistently weak results. "You're not stimulating him enough," she said. "A mind like his is special. It gets bored easily. It isn't motivated by this nonsense they teach at school." The man had pulled at his tie, shuffled his papers. He tried to explain to her that she might wish to consider the value of discipline, deadlines, of enforced bedtimes and rules. Things like that molded a person for the years to come. She shook her head, stood up to leave. "Thank you for your time, sir, but as his mother I know what's best. We will keep on as we are. Until he breaks a rule, you don't really have anything to complain of."

Afternoons she went out to the garage door, carrying a tray, using her elbow to knock on the wood's flaking paint.

"What?"

"It's just me. I brought Coke and biscuits."

The biscuits she made fresh for him, twice a week. He didn't eat the store-bought kind, said they tasted of cardboard. She made mostly sugar cookies or oat crunchies, sometimes chocolate fridge-cake bars, but never anything else. Those were the only kinds that he liked. Most days he said, "I'm busy. Just leave it outside." But sometimes he came to the door, blinking at her as he wiped his blackened hands on the overalls that she insisted he wear while working.

"There he is," she said. "The man of the future."

"Ah, Ma. Don't start with that now."

"Start what? I'm just saying I'm proud of you, my boy. You're what we need. Men like you who have ideas and work hard."

He took a biscuit, bit into it. "These are good. I like them when they're still a bit warm."

She felt a pang at the memory. Who had baked for him all these years? Who had cooked and washed and ironed and cleaned? He had been no more than a boy when he was forced to go away. He hadn't known a thing, not a thing about taking care of himself.

She squeezed his hand. "You've done well."

"Thanks."

"And here you are."

"Here I am."

"I knew they were wrong about you. All this time I knew it. I told them, 'No, not my boy, he didn't do those things.' I told them you were a good boy, a man of the future. You wouldn't do anything wrong. And I said, I always said you would come back to me. You would come and take care of me. You wouldn't let me die here, alone in a place like this."

Her voice cracked and he brought the straw to her lips again, holding it there while she drank what was left in the cup. "I've been calling for water for so long," she said. "Calling and calling, and nobody ever comes."

PART TWO

Deidre

She was not dressed, had not even thought of it, when the call came over the intercom: a policeman to pick her up.

"Should I send him through to your room?" Winston asked.

"Nah, let him wait. I'll be down in a minute."

She sighed, drew her arms above her head, looked at the television, where a local soap was playing. It was a repeat of the previous evening's episode, the same scene that had bored her then and made her pick up the phone. Monica had answered after several rings. "Hello? Hello? Oh hi, Mom. Sorry, I left my phone upstairs and I had to run for it."

"You shouldn't be running like that."

"Oh please, I'm fine." Then, "Hold on a sec." Calling away from the phone, "It's my mom. You start, I'm coming now." Back to Deidre, "Sorry, we were just sitting down to dinner."

"Well, I won't keep you. I just wanted to hear how the little thing's doing."

"The little thing is the size of a peanut and is killing me. The first few hours of the day are terrible, really terrible."

"Sorry, darling. But it'll get better, right?"

"Oh, it's not a problem. I'm managing. I mean, that's one of the great things about us working for ourselves—we can choose our hours."

"And James is being good to you, treating you well?"

"Of course, poor man! He's actually doing most of the work. And he's so excited about the baby that every time I burp, he's on the phone to his mom and she comes round with ginger tea and all sorts of things for me."

"Now you're making me jealous."

"Listen, you know the offer still stands. We want you to come, and we'll pay. It's not a problem. We'll fly you over whenever you want. Just say when. Like, after the baby's born, or come before even. Whenever you want."

She tried to imagine herself on a plane, the way it seemed in movies and TV programs. But could not get beyond a vision of herself, sitting trapped in her hospital bed on that long ward, without a leg, without crutches, with nothing at all but the sky wide and endless all around her and no way of escaping it. She said, "I don't know. It'll be too difficult. I'll just end up being one more thing for you to worry about and make problems for you."

"No, honestly, you won't. I want you to see my life here, and to finally meet James. And the baby, of course. I want you to meet the baby. These are things we should be sharing. I mean, I'm having a baby! I need you here to be part of it."

She thought about what it had been like for her. A baby in her arms that had not been expected or looked for. Nothing prepared, nothing in the house that might be useful. And so little money then, only a small income from investments her father had made with his retrenchment package. Not enough for a baby, hardly enough for the three of them, not when there were hospital bills to pay. He'd had to go to the Salvation Army's charity shop near the Magistrates' Court in Wynberg, where an elderly lady with plastic earrings helped him to pick out a few onesies, several cloth nappies, and an almost new set of baby bottles. There'd been no crib, the lady saying it was a pity, as they'd had a very nice one sell just the week before, but if he left his number she could call if another came in. He'd thanked her, explaining that there could be no waiting; it was needed immediately. She said again what a pity it was, that she wished she had one for him, she really did. Hopefully he could find one elsewhere, good luck to him, and he was welcome to come again anytime.

He'd gone on to the dumping ground near the racecourse, called over one of the men who came in each morning from the informal settlements, men who gathered on the road nearby, waiting for someone to pick them up and give them a day's work. The man helped her father search out several planks of wood and place them in the boot of the car. He was middle-aged, wore a khaki blazer and a brown slouch hat.

"You're new to Cape Town?" her father asked.

The man nodded. "I come for job. There jobs here because we vote. But I find no job."

"You should go home. There's no jobs for anyone now. Just go home." He took out his wallet, gave all the coins he had, close to ten rand, and the man made a bowl of his hands, ducking a little.

There were no tools in the house either, all of them wrecked in the explosion, and he'd had to borrow what he could from ex-colleagues and friends, using a small hand-saw he'd been told he could "just take, I don't use it any-more and you need it more than me," to cut the planks down to size. Afterward he sanded them by hand on a plastic garden table that stood beneath an awning at the back of the house. He built a crib and painted it, leaving it on a patch of concrete where the sun fell hot in the afternoon and where it would dry quickly.

Another day he came with cardboard boxes, carrying them down the long passage to Ross's room. The door was closed, and he had to put them down before he could turn the handle. Inside he found his wife, sitting at the desk. She looked up when he came in, not at his face, but behind, into the passage, at the boxes. "He might come back," she said. He nodded, took them to Deidre's room instead. He helped her to fill them with the things of her younger years, then shifted the bed and desk against the wall to make space for the crib. He said, "Actually, it's better this way, isn't it? Better to have her close." Later he'd brought in the crib, smelling of fresh paint, and an old, narrow armchair from the lounge with a faded flower pattern, and an embroidered cushion that her grandmother had made. He set the chair by the window, mentioned that the view wasn't a bad one. A bougainvillea against a wall, the neighbor's roof, a lemon tree, and beyond that the mountain, which seemed to be set in motion by the sun's hand, carried nearer or further at different hours of the day.

She had only just begun walking again by then, having refused it for all those months, refusing, too, the prosthesis that she had been offered and that everyone had tried to talk her into. Even so, she had no difficulty in the room, managing without crutches. She could lift Monica and sit in the chair without the need for walking. She'd doze there, her nose on the baby's soft head, waking more often than not to her father coming in, asking, "Is she ready for her bottle?" then feeding her himself, and saying often, as though he had only just thought of it, "One door closes and another one opens."

Several times her mother came to the doorway, but did not enter. Only stood looking in, turning her head a little, listening for something.

"What is it, Trudy?" her father said, walking over with the baby. "Do you want to hold her?"

She shook her head, put up a hand to keep him back. But, "Is she sick?" she asked once. "I think she might be sick. She never cries."

"That means she's happy."

"Do you think so?"

"Yes, of course. Why wouldn't she be?"

Now, in the morning's brittle light, Deidre stared at the TV for another minute, then swore and rose from the bed. She began to go through a pile of clothes on the floor. Nothing was clean, everything smelling of body and heat. She found a top, a short skirt, kept on her underwear from the previous day. The intercom rang once abruptly, stopped, rang again, longer. "I'm coming," she said, sitting on the edge of the bed to put on her shoe. "I'm fucking coming."

Winston opened the door for her with a smile. "Someone's a VIP today." He nodded at the handicapped parking bay where a police car stood. The officer was leaning in on the passenger side to adjust the seat. He'd pushed it all the way back, looked up when Deidre said, "You here for me?"

"Mrs. van Deventer?"

"Miss."

"Yes, of course. Good morning, Miss van Deventer. I'm Detective Sergeant Mabombo." He gestured at the seat. "Is it okay like this?"

"I'm a cripple, not a giant. Just toss these in the back." She shoved the crutches at him, holding on to the doorframe to balance herself, and sat down. She began adjusting the seat, grunting at the effort so that Mabombo might hear that she had been inconvenienced—by the seat, by him, by the whole business. He got in and waited for her.

"Ready?"

"Uh-huh."

"Could you put on your seatbelt, please?"

"Ja, I'm doing it."

Mabombo started the engine, reversed with care. There was no dirt inside the car, nothing to show whether it was used often or not, though it had been dusty enough on the outside. There was a green cardboard circle hanging from the rearview mirror, a scent of pine, and wrapped sweets in the cupholder between the seats.

"Can I have one?" she asked.

"Please, help yourself."

She did, taking three, unwrapping them all at once and then not knowing what to do with the papers. She put them on her lap. Mabombo was clean too, smelling of cologne. She turned her head, tried to sniff her armpit, but could smell nothing besides her own foul breath. She took some more sweets, chewed them a little, moved them around her mouth, across her teeth and tongue.

"So, listen," she said, "what's this about anyway? That woman, I forget her name, she wouldn't tell me anything."

"Detective Constable Xaba."

"Jesus, how do you expect me to say that?"

Mabombo smiled politely. "It's only a matter of a small click at the side of the mouth, like this." He made the sound a few times.

She tried it once, twice, then, "I'll just call her Zaba. With a name like that she must be used to it by now."

"I imagine she is, though it always makes a difference when someone tries."

Deidre began looking in her bag. "Can I smoke?"

"No, I'm afraid that isn't allowed."

She took two more sweets from the cupholder. There were only three left. She put both in her mouth, chewing as she looked out of the window. It was a long time since she'd last passed this way, though it wasn't so far from where she lived now. At one time it had been marshland, but in recent years it had been taken over by an informal settlement, extending right up to the edge of the highway. Shack upon shack that seemed to have emerged from an abundance of smog and detritus, the verge gray with cast-off plastic and unwanted things, and at the edges the hasty footsteps of children kicking something that ought to have been a ball.

"Jesus, look at that. They keep coming closer and closer. I mean, did you see on the news the other day about that fire that went through one of these places? Not this one; one of those ones there on the way to Stellenbosch. Millions of liters of water wasted on people like this who don't even pay for it, no tax or anything. It should've just been left to burn."

Mabombo cleared his throat. "It was near Kommetjie, I believe, not Stellenbosch. And they used seawater to put out the fire, since that is the only water available these days."

Deidre didn't reply, chewed noisily.

"You know, people died in that fire," Mabombo said. "One of them was a baby."

She shifted in her seat, pulled at the strap of the bag

around her neck. "Well, no. Not babies. That's not right. I'd never wish death on a baby."

"No, ma'am."

"You have children?"

He gave a half smile. "My wife and I are waiting to adopt. We're on a list."

"Good. That's a good thing to do. My daughter is adopted."

"Really?"

"Ja. But she's not here. She lives in London. She's married to some guy from Jamaica, or, no, I think it's Barbados. I always forget. Anyway, she's been to visit Barbados four times, met all his cousins and aunts and all that, but she's never come home. Not once in thirteen years."

"Oh, I'm sorry to hear that."

She looked at him, then at her lap, shrugging. "Ah well, that's the way it is. They all like to leave, hey, the young ones. They want the whole world. Here is never enough for them. But look at me, I didn't go anywhere. I stayed here."

"You didn't ever want to take a gap year or something after you finished school?"

"Nah, I was in the hospital a lot of the time for this shit." She waved at her stump.

"I see."

He turned in to a side street, parked the car, said, "Right, here we are."

She peered out of the window, thought it was a joke, gave a short breath of laughter through her nose. "Okay," she said, waiting for him to turn the key and drive on. But he was already unbuckling his seatbelt, patting his jacket to make sure he had his phone. "Wait, where are we?"

"Your house. It's Sixteen Protea Street, right?"

The entire block on either side, and more beyond, back toward the mountain, had been demolished. There were no houses remaining, no trees or fences, only an uneven surface upon which great chunks of rubble had been flung, and about them shone cleavings of blue and green tiles from a swimming pool's edge. Her family hadn't had a pool, but the neighbors had, and sometimes, when they were still children, they waited for their mom to go off to one of her women's group meetings at the church and then climbed over the concrete wall to swim, grabbing noodles and boogie boards from the open shed while the neighbors' ancient Maltese barked at them from inside the house.

She closed her eyes against the sight. Hard to think of it now, that water. Hard to think of it with things the way they were, with the drought and with pools having stood empty for years already, gaping dryly across the land. In her throat, too, that old feeling once again, of thirst and want, and she gathered her saliva, tasting the sweetness of it, swallowing hard that the thirst might go away. But it remained, drew her deeper, taking her thoughts to other waters, to the public pool at Newlands, which had been left to fall apart. Not that it had ever been much of anything before, though she had only known it from the interschools swimming galas. All those teenagers in their uniforms, faces painted in school colors, screaming the cheers as though it mattered who won. Most of them away from the stands, near the toilets, making out with whoever they could find. Her first kiss had been like that. He'd still been wet from a race, his freckles dark against his pale cheeks and forehead.

She began to unbuckle her seatbelt, looked down at her lap, picked up the empty sweet wrappers that lay there, and placed them back in the cupholder. Wet freckled arms around her, smelling of chlorine and cheese Nik Naks. Memories tricking her, making her believe her childhood had been nothing but water, always water. Winters of storms and flooded streets, and in the summer the Super Tubes at Muizenberg, or the beach, or pool parties. And now this here in front of her. This dry upheaval that turned all of the past into a layer of dust, ready for the wind to lift and scatter.

"So, it's really happening, hey," she said to Mabombo.

"It looks like it."

"I never really thought it would, you know. I thought they'd fuck around with documents and shit for a few years and then just give it all back. But that's not going to happen anymore, is it?"

"No, I don't think so."

She nodded, sucked her lower lip. Two years of waiting to return home, and nothing now to come back to. Nothing left of any of it, apart from this hideous desolation, and shards of memory that didn't quite fit together. Returning from a walk with Monica, seeing her father at the gate in angry conversation with a Colored man. Another time, hearing him on the phone, speaking low about forced removals and land claims. And then nothing more, not another word about any of it for almost twenty-five years. By then he had been dead, and Monica long since gone away. Only herself and her mother to peer at the letter that arrived, trying to make sense of the fact that something final had happened, something final in a conversation in which they had not participated. The land would be taken. But it would not be returned to the Colored families who had once lived there. It would go to the state; this entire area was to be theirs, with its aquifers that ran deep underground.

Of course, the lawyer had said, of course they'd all be recompensed; the former inhabitants who had been so cruelly robbed in the past, and the current homeowners, who had certainly been ignorant of the land's history. But no money came. Temporary problems, they were told, only temporary problems. Until the financial situation was resolved, the homeowners would be generously relocated, free of charge, to comfortable living quarters nearby. When she'd first started going to the Nine Lives, the papers were full of the story. Ricardo calling across to her, "Oh, Deidre, here's something that will interest you," reading out what she already knew, that the contract for housing had gone to a friend of the president, a man who ran several old-age facilities and who couldn't get them filled because of the prices he asked. Now the rooms were occupied and the government was paying him as he laughed his way to the bank. "Always this nepotism and corruption. It's such a shame," Ricardo had said.

She looked out of the window again. There were bull-dozers and diggers on-site, none of them in motion. Work-ers sat on the edge of what had been a pavement, drinking from two-liter bottles of cheap fizzy drinks. They eyed the open land where a man in a hard hat was striding across to a woman in a gray pantsuit. The woman stood behind a stretch of police tape that marked out a large rectangle. She'd been talking to a uniformed officer, but she stepped away now, came forward to hear what the man wanted.

Mabombo opened the door for Deidre, said, "Just a mo-ment," as he went to the back for her crutches.

She could hear the conversation, the woman's voice cut-ting across the empty plot. "Your deadlines are irrelevant. This is a crime scene with an ongoing investigation. There is no compromise in this situation."

Then Mabombo was back, holding out the crutches for her. She took them, got out of the car, a sweet wrapper fall-ing from her lap. He bent to pick it up, put it in his pocket. "This way, please."

"Forget it." She jerked her head at the uneven terrain, the piles of debris. "There's no way I can walk on that."

Mabombo paused, looked at her, at the ground. "Yes, I see. Of course. Please, wait here a moment while I tell De-tective Constable Xaba that we're here."

"Ja, okay."

She took out a cigarette, began to smoke sulkily. Without trees or houses to block the view, the mountain appeared closer. As though it had taken a few steps forward in the years since she'd last been here, and grown in size. The sky, too, had grown. It came down on all sides, pressing its weight on her, with nothing to hold it up. Her throat began to panic at the burden, to flutter into a cough. She shook her head, struggling against the heaviness, the sky seeming to darken around her.

Then, from the near distance, the squeal of a train pulling into the station a few blocks down, and a prerecorded announcement over the loudspeaker. She sniffed, wiped her palm across her nose, rubbed it on her skirt. She waited for the familiarity to return, of the train leaving the station, the shunt, shunt, shunt as it moved on. Mornings, that sound waking her if the wind was in the right direction. And always the bells clanging, clanging, from the Catholic church around the corner, the one with the large crucified Christ in the garden. She and Ross daring one another to run up the slate path, touch his nailed foot, run back.

It had been a good place to live. A cul-de-sac, with nice people, nice children. But, after everything, they had become unpleasant, turning away from her parents and herself, going inside rather than saying hello or giving a nod. People they'd lived beside for almost twenty years, pretending not to know them. Yet they watched from their windows. Watched as she learned to crutch herself up and down the street, since the driveway was all bricks and rub-

bish still. Watched her complaining at the effort, watched
her dad say, "Come on, girl, just ten more meters, that's all.
Just ten more and we'll go inside." That humiliation on top
of everything else, of not being able to do it. Of being left
without a leg and not being able to fucking walk without
crying or screaming or having a fucking fit. Throwing the
crutches away from herself, lying down on the damp road,
and bawling, "I won't do it, Daddy, I won't. I'm tired. I'm
too tired."

"Deidre, love, come on, let's try again."

"No, I'm too tired. Just leave me alone."

But he hadn't left her. He'd picked her up, carried her
inside, with all the neighborhood peering out at her, and the
fucking crutches still in the road for anyone to take or drive
over or chuck into the garbage, where they could stay and
rot for all she cared.

Mabombo returned with the woman in the pantsuit.
Like him, she was pristine, her blouse crisp. She frowned as
Deidre tossed her cigarette butt in the gutter, said, "Thank
you for coming, Miss van Deventer. I'm sorry about the in-
convenient terrain. I should have considered that."

"What's this about?"

"Miss van Deventer, am I correct in saying that your
brother, uh," she paused to take a notebook out of her
pocket, glanced at an open page, "Rossouw Bernard van
Deventer, was a member of a pro-apartheid group in the
nineteen nineties?"

"God, not this shit again. It wasn't like that, okay."

"But it is true that he was building bombs as part of a plot to blow up certain voting centers during the 1994 elections and that those bombs were built on this property, where one of them was detonated on the night of," she looked at the notebook again, "twentieth of April 1994?"

"That was just a accident, that's all. He was fooling around with some stuff, just messing around like any teenage boy, and then there was this explosion. That's it."

"I—excuse me for saying so—I understand that it was in that explosion that you lost your leg."

"Ja, and?"

"And that eyewitnesses reported seeing Rossouw fleeing the scene immediately afterward."

"Of course he ran away! He was afraid. Wouldn't you be?"

"Did your brother ever return, ever try to make contact?"

"Why are you bringing all this up now? I mean, what does it matter? Did you find another bomb or something?"

"No, ma'am, we didn't find any bombs. I'm afraid that what we've found is the remains of several bodies."

"What? What do you mean bodies?" She looked across at the uniformed officer, the police tape demarcating the area where a flower bed had been in the back garden. "Wait a minute. What are you saying? You found them on our property?"

"That's correct, yes. We have, so far, located three bodies on this property, dated at present as having been buried at

some point in the mid to late nineties, though we hope to
have a more specific time frame soon."

"Three?"

"Yes, three." Xaba paused, returned the notebook to her
jacket pocket. "I'm sorry to have to tell you this, but they
were infants. Children under the age of two."

"No, no, no, no. That's wrong. There's—it's not—I
mean, there's no way. No way. That's not Ross. He was a
dickhead, yes, he really was. I can tell you that. But he had
nothing to do with anything like this. Really. No way.
You've got it wrong."

"Miss van Deventer, I understand your feelings, but at
this point we're only inquiring—"

"Look, you've made a mistake. You need to find the
family that lived here before us. The place was a mess when
my parents got it. There was rubbish and heaps of stuff everywhere, like a dump, like a actual dump. I'm telling you."

"Ma'am, I assure you—"

"No, no, I'm telling you, find that family. Their name is
Hendricks. Hendricks with a 'd' in the middle, okay. Write
that down. Where's your notebook? Write that down. Hendricks. You find them, they're the ones you're looking for."

"Maybe—"

"There's documents showing they wanted the place
back. They said they'd been forced out by the old government and they said they wanted it back, it was theirs. I'm
telling you there are documents, I've seen them, I found
them in my dad's stuff when you people came and forced us

out. Is that all you do, force people out? Just force people out of their homes. It's always this same bullshit, this same fucking bullshit."

"Miss van Deventer, I understand that this is upsetting for you, but right now we are only asking preliminary questions. We'd like you to look at a few items that the team has found on the property. Would that be all right?"

She shook her head. "You're not listening to me. Find that fucking family. They're the ones you're looking for. They wanted their place back and that's what they did, they planted all that shit there to make us look bad. I'm serious. You need to go and fucking find them."

"Yes, ma'am. I assure you that we'll be looking into all potential avenues. But I can see that you are distressed at present, so perhaps you can look at the items another day and Detective Sergeant Mabombo can take you home now?"

"So that's it? You bring me all the way here, tell me a load of fucking bullshit, and now you're trying to chase me away?"

"Miss van Deventer, I thank you very much for your assistance today, but we will continue this conversation at another time."

Deidre watched Xaba walk away, back across the empty plot to where the officer stood, watched her shake her head, say something low. The officer glanced at Deidre, turned his head, spoke to Xaba, nodded. On the pavement's edge the workers still sat, some of them leaning back now, bored.

They talked among themselves, empty bottles scattered around them. The breeze picked one up, made it tumble noisily into the street before one of the men stood, tried to retrieve it, missed, then grabbed again, one leg in the air, losing his balance a little. A few of his companions laughed, made comments, and he laughed too, sat back down with a smile. It seemed to Deidre that the tumble of the bottle, the laughter and words were all meant for her. All of this mockery coming at her from sky and mountain, from every part of the demolished plots, everything reaching toward her with suffocating scorn. The tumbling bottle, the laughter, the man standing on one leg under the oppressive sky, and she called out, to Xaba, to them all, "Did you bring me here just to make fun of me, is that it? I'm a joke, a fucking joke."

Mabombo put an arm out, came near but didn't touch. "Let me take you home."

"Listen to me," but she had to pause, had to bite down against the pulsing in her throat. "Listen, it was a rubbish tip when my dad got the place. He always said that. Those exact words: it was a rubbish tip. He cleared it all by himself, made it nice. I know you can't see that now, the way it is, but I have photos somewhere. I can bring them to show you and you'll see."

"Yes, ma'am."

He helped her into the car as before, reminded her about her seatbelt, then went around and got into the driver's seat.

"Are you all right?" he said.

She looked out at the destroyed earth, the heaps of rubble, the darkening sky. "They were babies?"

"Yes."

She put her head back, closed her eyes. There was the laughter, the tumbling bottle, the sky pushing her down, squashing her with its dark weight. Again and again those things, those sounds, again and again. And the babies dead in the ground. She thought of them being held, thought of a newborn in her arms. The scent of powder and milk, the rhythm of quick little breaths.

Beside her, Mabombo turned the key in the ignition. She opened her eyes, looked down, saw that she had raised her arms, had brought them close, was cradling air.

"Why did you bring me here?" she said. "Why the fuck did you make me come back?"

All morning her throat had been fretting, until provoked at last into its full, dark urgency, into a terror that her thirst would not be quenched. She was dizzy with it, standing here in the gutter on the side of the main road where Mabombo had dropped her as she shouted, "Anywhere, I don't care, anywhere, just let me out!" Then heaving that urgency dryly into her mouth, Mabombo watching uncertainly behind.

Her crutches straddled the gutter and pavement, yet in her sickness it seemed as though a ditch ran beneath her feet. Seemed as though she had remained in Protea Street and had accompanied Xaba across the uneven demolition site to the cordoned-off rectangle where the hydrangeas had once grown. She looked down into the black earth, down into its tangle of roots and fragments, searching for the remains she had been told about, trying to pick out any small bones that might be lost within. But nothing, nothing.

Then a hand on her shoulder, startling her out of the dark and back into the terror. "Will you at least get onto the pavement, Miss van Deventer," said Mabombo, "then I will leave you alone, if you are sure you don't want me here."

"Just go away; I'm done with you people." Even so, she stepped up, the movement difficult, causing her to sway back a little, to think she might fall, her head and throat continuing to pulse their nausea.

She knew now that there could be no waiting, that something was needed at once. She felt in her bag, first with one hand, then the other, feeling the crumbs and dirt. No singles there, no coins either. And nothing left on her debit card.

She turned back toward the police car, began to call to Mabombo, but he was already pulling away. No one else nearby, only the passing cars. She thought of stepping into the road, waving down a motorist and begging for money, saying she needed it for the hospital or medicine or something like that. Something important. Something that could not be refused.

But not yet that humiliation. Not yet that.

Nothing now but to turn once more to the gutter, walking slowly above it, her eyes alert, following it toward the end of the long block, knowing that it would come, that soon it would come. And then it was there and she crouched down as best she could, her thigh shaking with the effort, the crutches ready to fall, and clawed the thing out of the dirt. She rose again, blowing the grit off it, pushing the filter end back into shape where it had been flattened. She brought it to her lips, lit it with unsteady hands, her first taste of it dull with sand and age, and then the warm inhalation of someone else's breath. The sickness was still fresh within her, fresh enough that she became momentarily confused, half-certain that this was not a cigarette end, that this was not a gutter. That it was once more the ditch, and that what she had in her mouth was the dying breath of a child, caught in a baby's bone.

She stood outside the Nine Lives, smoking the last of several entjies she had picked up along the way. From time to time she let her hand slip into her bag, checked that they were still there—a five rand coin and a couple of smaller ones. 5.60 rand she had. 5.60 rand. The R5 weighty in her hand, feeling like it filled her palm, like she was rich. It was money. She had money.

She tossed the entjie, had tried to get too much from it, her tongue bitter now with the burnt filter, and went inside, going to the right end of the bar, the dark corner, away from where Ricardo and Steven sat. She waved Isaac over, put the coins on the counter with dirty fingers. "What can I get for this?"

He looked at the coins, then at her face. "Come on, don't do this to me."

"Please." She spoke low, pushed the coins forward. "Please, just something."

He glanced around, wiped the coins off the bar into his hand. "Half a shot, that's all I can do."

"Can it be three quarters? Please. Just this one time. I just need something today."

He shook his head. "For fuck's sake, Deidre, I could lose my job." But he poured to the top of the shot glass, turning his back afterward so that he would not see her grab it and swallow it in one.

The nausea began to lift at once, her throat calming to a slow flutter. "Ah thanks, man. Thanks."

He still had his back to her, spoke fiercely over his shoulder. "Just sort yourself out. This can't happen again."

She walked away quietly, half-giddy with her achievement, greeting Ricardo and Steven, stopping to ask how they were, then went out into the unlit corridor and pushed open the door to the ladies' loo. She didn't often use it, but it was kept clean enough, wiped down with bleach and vinegar a few times a day, and flushed once at night with gray water. She sat down over the bowl that was brown with other people's piss. Nothing came; she was holding herself too tight. Already the thrill of the drink was leaving her, the dark nausea settling in again. She had to make herself breathe out, once, then twice, before the urine came. Only a few drops, burning where they touched her. She wiped, threw the paper in the bin. The toilet roll was half-empty, but it was the good kind, two-ply. She took it from the hook on the wall, flattened it a little, placed it in her bag. At the basin she pumped sanitizer onto her hands, rubbing them together until it evaporated, though her skin felt coated, less clean than before, her nails still black from the gutter.

When she came out of the bathroom, Marvin was on the stairs, holding the old wooden banister, and talking to a man a few steps below.

"Hey, Trevor!" she said. "Where the hell you been?"

He had been a regular, coming in every evening after work for a single beer, staying long enough for a chat, a laugh. But he'd retired at the end of the previous year and hadn't been round much since then.

"Hey, Deidre, nice to see you. Howzit?"

"Not good, man. Anyway, I thought we'd be seeing more of you, not less."

"What can I say, retirement's keeping me busy."

"Doing what?"

"I'm helping out at a charity."

She gave a short laugh. "Jesus."

"No, really, it's great. I love it. Actually, that's why I'm here. I came to talk to the boss," he pointed upstairs in the direction of the office, "about letting us have some cardboard boxes from the bottle store."

"Hope they're for packing up all the rubbish that comes in here," said Marvin, still on the stairs. "It's getting worse, you know. I mean, really, you should see the people we get in here sometimes, like they crawled out of a homeless shelter or something."

"What the fuck, Marvin," said Deidre. "You can't say shit like that. It's offensive. It's fucking offensive. You think you're so fancy in your Pep Stores jeans and Shoprite shoes? Mr. Rich and Fancy, is that what you think you are in that shit, huh? You're the one that should be put in a box and taken away."

"Ah, relax, Deidre. You always have to be so fucking dramatic."

"Ja, maybe I do, because no one else stands up to you, that's why."

Trevor put up his hand. "Okay, guys, that's enough. Deidre, let's go this way."

He led her down the passage until they were standing near the entrance to the bottle store.

She looked back at the staircase, but Marvin had gone. "I really hate that guy. I mean, the things he says . . ."

"Just ignore him. He's not worth getting upset about."

"I know, but he just gets to me, every time. Really gets to me." She took a breath, shook her head. "Anyway, now that you're here, you can buy me a drink. I'm having a really bad day."

He looked at his phone. "It's not even lunchtime yet."

"So, who's counting?"

"Well, listen, it's too early in the day for me, but I've been on the go since five and I'm starving. I bet you haven't eaten yet either."

"I had some sweets."

"That doesn't count. Come on, let's go to that fish and chips shop around the corner. I'm buying."

"I don't like fish."

He smiled, put his hand on her shoulder again. "Ah, Deidre, why do you have to be so difficult all the time?"

Trevor stood back, waited for her to enter. He approached one of two white plastic tables and pulled out a matching chair for her to sit on while he went up to the counter to place their order.

It was her first time inside the place, though she'd passed it often enough, had been able to smell the warmth of frying that hung over the block most days. The walls, floor, and counter were covered in pale blue tiles, a few of them embossed with the same gulping orange and green fish. One of the walls had been decorated with hundreds of newspaper cuttings, most yellowing, a few newer. There were cartoons—*Madam & Eve, Zapiro*—making fun of the government, the endless loadshedding, and the water crisis. Articles about service delivery protests, a fun day at a nearby preschool to raise money for new educational equipment. A faded image of piglets abandoned at the SPCA and put up for adoption.

She reached across to a small clear plastic bowl in the middle of the table, took out a packet of brown sugar. She tried to fold it over, once, twice, but couldn't get it to bend, then tore it open, let some of the grains spill onto the table. She pressed a finger into them, lifted them to her mouth, swallowed, glaring at the wall with its curling scraps. The shop was too bright, the lights stronger than they needed to be. And everything this strange pale blue, reflecting off the glass doors, coming back at her as sharp as sunlight. She shouldn't have come.

Then Trevor was back. "Sorry, sorry, I was just having a quick chat. But I'm here now, all yours," and he placed two purple cans on the table between them.

"What's this?"

He laughed, wiping the tops with a paper serviette, and passed one across to her. "Fanta grape. I know, it's childish, but I thought they might be fun. You only find crazy flavors in small places like this nowadays. You never see it at Pick n Pay or Checkers. Anyway, you said you were having a bad day. Maybe this'll cheer you up."

She held up the can, turned it around, before pulling the tab. There was a hiss of gas, a strong artificial scent, overly sweet. "God, I haven't had one of these in years. I didn't even know they still made them."

"Me too. That's why I got them. Who says we're too old for having adventures, huh? Cheers!"

They touched cans, drank, Trevor taking a large gulp and gasping. "Just as terrible as I remember." Then another. "Is my tongue purple yet?"

Deidre sipped, let it stay in her mouth a moment before swallowing. "It's funny how the taste of something stupid like this can just do something to you."

"Like what?"

"I don't know, I suppose it can almost, like, pick you up and put you somewhere else, like put you right inside a memory."

"Ja? What are you remembering?"

"Ah, I don't really know. It's not much of a memory. I mean, it's not anything special."

"Tell me anyway. I want to hear."

She took another sip, put the can down on the table, keeping her hand around it. "Well, it's not something I usually talk about, but my brother, Ross, he and I went to different schools when we were young. He was in Rutherford, up there near the rugby stadium, you know."

He nodded. "Good school."

"Ja, but I went just near our house to Mountain View. My dad used to drop Ross at school on his way to work, and my mom picked him up again in the afternoon. But I was really close, so I just walked. Anyway, I used to play hockey and tennis and do stuff like that after school, and I had this friend Tanya who did everything with me. Like if I wore my hair in a side pony then she did it too, or if she rolled her socks down then I would do the same, you know."

"Ja, best friends."

"Exactly. And Tanya lived kind of close to us, so we used

to walk home together after sport or choir or drama or whatever. And the thing about Tanya was that she always had some money on her, which was something I never had because I didn't get pocket money or anything like that. Anyway, so we'd be walking home and we'd stop at that café in Main Road near where the framing place is now, you know the one, what's it called? It's still there."

"Budget Cafe?"

"Budget, right. So, we'd stop there and get something with her money to share. Like Nik Naks or bubble gum, or this stuff," she held up the can, "and we'd drink it together. And that's it. That's the memory. Sharing a can of Fanta grape after school."

"Are you still in touch with her?"

"Nah. At the end of grade eight my brother failed and he had to stay back a year. My mom said it was because he was being bullied, but I don't think that's really what was going on. The point is, I got taken out of Mountain View and had to go to Rutherford with him, be in the same class, sit next to him, you know. Even though he was a year older than me, I had to look after him."

"Really? But could you at least still play sports and do all that other stuff?"

She shook her head. "Ross wanted to go home straight after school and my mom said she wasn't going to make two trips to pick me up later if I stayed for other things."

"So, you just had to give it all up? Your activities, your school, your friend, your Fanta grape."

Deidre shrugged. "She was pretty old-fashioned. That's just the way it was in our family."

The man at the counter called their number and Trevor pushed back his chair, went across to pick up the food. He returned, already unwrapping the greasy paper around the double portion of chips, and placed it in the middle of the table, then opened up his parcel of battered fish. "Go ahead." He nodded at the chips. "Do what you like to them. I eat them with mayo, mustard, tomato sauce, anything you like. I don't mind."

She put on salt and pepper, vinegar, poured a little tomato sauce from a red squeeze bottle. "So, what's this charity you were talking about?"

He reached for a serviette, wiped his mouth and fingertips. "Oh, it's really great. We do work in the informal settlements and on the Flats helping with water-wise community vegetable gardens, and we organize water to be taken to the old or sick or disabled because, as you must know yourself, it's hard for them to do the collecting for themselves."

She looked at her leg, then picked up the can, drank again. "Nice."

"It is. It really is. I mean, it's great to be helping people and to be involved. You should come and check it out some time. Anyone is welcome."

She took a chip, dipped it in tomato sauce, put it in her mouth. "Thanks, but I don't really think it's my kind of thing."

"No? What is your kind of thing?"

"I don't know. Nothing really."

"Did you ever have a job?"

"I raised my daughter. That's a job."

"You don't have to tell me. I have five children."

"Five? That's a lot."

"Ja, well, I was married twice. And divorced twice too. And you?"

"Nah, never married, never divorced."

He took a handful of chips, put them next to the fish, ate them one by one.

"I wasn't lazy or anything like that," she said.

"Sorry?"

"I mean about working. I wanted to study to be a nurse or a dental assistant, something like that. But I was eighteen when I lost my leg. It was in the middle of my matric year and so I never got to finish high school."

"And you didn't want to do it later, like night school or something?"

"Nah, by then I had my daughter and that took up all my time."

He pointed at her stump with a chip. "You weren't given the choice of a prosthesis?"

"I was. But it didn't—I didn't like the way it felt. My leg was gone and they wanted to replace it with this thing. It wasn't right. I didn't want it. The whole thing was such bullshit. Ah, look, I've had a tough morning. I don't want to talk about this today."

"Sorry. Is there anything I can do for you?"

She wanted to say, "Ja, buy me a box of wine." Instead, she grabbed the Fanta, drank it down too fast. Once more this dark sickness upon her, the taste of her childhood a rotting thing that she couldn't swallow away, and, as she placed the can on the table, that other child, the dead one whose breath she had inhaled, came out from the dark and gasped within her.

Trudy

She woke to a nurse, the fat one whose name was something like Beauty or Pretty even though she was far from it. She was wheeling a tray table into place over the bed, saying, "Morning, Mrs. van Deventer, my dear, how are you today? Did you sleep well? Look at what I've got for you, delicious breakfast."

She turned her head from the smell of processed meat, tried to pull her neck in below the covers, but the nurse said, "Let's get you sitting up, my dear," and adjusted the tilt of the bed, maneuvering Trudy's body until she was sitting upright against two pillows.

She looked past the nurse's back at the window, the vacant chair, looked across at the open door of the bathroom. "Where's Ross?"

"What's that, my dear?"

"My son. Ross. Wasn't he here when you came in? He

said he was going to stay the night. Did he leave? Did you make him leave?"

"It's too early for visitors now. I'm sure he'll be here later."

"Did you make him leave?"

"Don't worry about that now, my dear. Let's eat your breakfast."

Trudy turned her head again, pressed her mouth into her shoulder.

"Not hungry? Not even for a bit of scrambled egg with Viennas? And look, we have a slice of tomato today, isn't that nice? Come, dear, open up." The nurse took hold of Trudy's chin, pushed a forkful of the eggs into her mouth. They were overcooked, cold. The nurse waited for her to swallow, pushed in more.

Trudy chewed slowly, shook her head at the approach of the next one. "Enough."

The nurse placed the fork on the tray, tutted. "All right, my dear, but don't complain to me when you're hungry later, okay?"

"I won't be. My son's bringing me lunch."

"That's nice, my dear. So, let's have your tea now."

Trudy shook her head. "I don't want tea. Where's Ross? Go find him. Tell him I'm waiting for him."

"Now now, Mrs. van Deventer, you're not starting with your nonsense again, are you? You're not being difficult again, mm? Are we going to have to call the matron?"

"Where's Ross?" she said, but let the nurse put the cup

to her lips. The tea was thick, as always, with powdered milk. Difficult to get down, though she managed half of it before pushing it away.

The nurse returned it to the tray table, wheeled it away from the bed. She came back smiling. "Do you feel like trying to get up today to use the commode, my dear? We can take a nice little trip to the bathroom. Or I can wheel it out here if you don't think you can make it that far."

"My son," said Trudy, pointing at the doorway. "Bring him back."

"I see it's going to be one of those days, Mrs. van Deventer."

She went into the bathroom, came out with a bedpan, placed it underneath Trudy and said, "Just tell me when you're finished, okay?" then went to sit in the chair, her arms crossed in front of her.

But Trudy could do nothing, had her eyes on the door. She didn't want Ross to enter, find her like this, in this position. Yet let him come back, only let him come back. The rest could wait.

The nurse removed the empty bedpan, then stripped her, gave her a quick once-over with a wet cloth, starting at her face, then all the way down to her feet before swapping over to a different cloth to clean between her legs. When she was finished, she put the same clothes back on Trudy, brushed her hair, coming so close that her breasts pressed against Trudy's arm and side.

"You're hurting me. Get off. Get off the bed."

"You're so fussy today, my dear. Just hold on another second."

Trudy could feel the hair fluffing around her forehead and ears, her scalp smarting at the touch of the bristles. "That's fine," she said. "That's enough."

"Okay, there we go. Now you're ready for any visitor that might come." The nurse moved her bulk away from the bed, returned with a little yellow plastic compact from the pocket of her cardigan that lay over the back of a chair. She held it out for Trudy to look into.

"What's that?" she said, taking hold of the mirror, bringing it close to her face.

"What's that? Oh, you're silly today, my dear, very silly. That's you."

"Me?"

She took in the bordered circle of skin and wrinkles. It was a face, yes, she could see that now, but a face missing most of its features. Where was the mouth, where the eyes? In their place were only folds of skin marked by large brown flecks and deep furrows. She glanced across at the nurse, saw her face with its cheeks, mouth, eyes, all the things expected of a face, even a fat, ugly one. The nurse smiled, nodded encouragement. "Yes, dear, that's you. Look how nice you look. Your hair's as soft as a baby's. So lovely."

She'd planned to ask for her teeth today, to meet Ross with a smile. But she couldn't now, not after seeing that she had nothing at all left of herself.

She dozed, waking in the past, half dream, half memory. In the old Woolworths there in Wynberg, looking at dresses. They'd already been in Ackermans, bought shoes for Ross and a new pair of trousers because he was two years old and always growing, growing, those long legs of his carrying him all over the place so that she had to keep ahold of his hand in public. There was a pretty dress, chiffon with pleats on the skirt, though she had nowhere to wear it to, a dress like that. Too fancy for church. She thought about trying it on anyway, had the hanger in her hand, when Deidre began to fret. Trudy returned the dress to the rack, let go of Ross's hand, bent down to the pram, and put the pacifier back in Deidre's mouth. She adjusted her socks and shoes, felt to see if her nappy was full. "You're fine," she said, touching a finger to her cheek. "Just a bit tired from all the excitement. Go to sleep, you can sleep. We're leaving soon, isn't that right, Ross?"

But Ross wasn't there anymore. She stood up, looked around at the nearby rails of clothes, called his name, then another time, knowing already, certain of it, that he'd been kidnapped. There was no other explanation. There could be no other. He'd been taken.

Just the previous year, a few months after Deidre's birth, there had been uprisings in the north of the country, in Soweto. Violent protests against the government. The police had acted and some people had died, teenagers and children. The Blacks were angry, threatening revenge, and "no one is safe, not any of us," said the ladies from the women's group. Lucy Pienaar showed them a revolver her husband had given her and which she carried in her handbag at all times. But Paul had refused when Trudy asked for one, and now she was here, and Ross had been taken.

She ran to the entrance that opened onto Main Road with all its people and traffic, and oh God he'd been taken into that, into a car or onto a motorbike, or in a bag on someone's back, and he was gone.

But, no, said the guard. There'd been no one through those doors in the last five minutes. Not a soul. The child must still be in the shop. His face, that guard, his large nose with its black hairs, his hat and tie, unpolished shoes, all of that appearing now as they had back then, exactly so. Her own blouse too, her stockinged heels slipping in her shoes, Deidre's curls, the feel of the pram's handles. And he was gone, she knew he was gone.

Only, he was not gone. They had found him in the ladies' changing room, trying on hats in front of the full-length mirror. His little face smiling under a navy blue satin brim with a polka-dotted veil. She had pulled him to her, held him close, remaining like that for a while, the dream shifting around them, moving her from one memory into another. This one she knew well, had visited often. Here she was in her nightgown, under the covers, half asleep in the dark, and here was the sound of the radio playing in Ross's room, even though he'd said he would try going to bed earlier. But he liked this show, the one from 10:00 P.M. to midnight that played the latest music. Heavy metal, he called it. Horrible to her ears, but he didn't like to miss it, and it didn't matter so much, staying up late from time to time.

Paul snoring in the lounge. He'd fallen asleep reading the paper again, would wake in the morning with pain in his back and neck if she didn't go and call him. She opened her eyes, was about to get out of bed, before hearing the creak of Deidre's bedroom door opening. Trudy waited to see if she was going to the bathroom. But the girl tiptoed past, through to the kitchen. She could hear the bolt being pulled back, the back door opening softly, closing.

They'd caught her before, she and Paul, caught her sneaking out. They'd told her, made it perfectly clear, that she wasn't allowed to see this boyfriend of hers anymore. He was too old for her, already in his twenties, what did he want with a high school girl? "And," she'd said, "and, really, what kind of a man is he? Just some white trash from

Gabriel Estate." Maybe if he had a job, or if he was study-ing, maybe then they could understand, but a man like that was not what they had in mind for her. "You deserve bet-ter," she'd said. "What about the nice boys at school? We pay enough for you to go to that place."

But now it was starting up again. She could hear the careful footsteps outside her window, and from the top of the road the sound of a motorbike approaching, stopping. Trudy stayed where she was. She wasn't going to make a scene for all the neighbors to hear. Let Deidre go, and see what happened to her life. Let her go and see.

The explosion seemed less loud in the dream. As though all sound had dulled to a sensation only. There was her body, jolted away from itself, her heart fast in her stomach, ready to vomit, the slow blur of glass coming at her, and a great exhaling heat. She rose, hunched with nausea, and fumbled for the bedside lamp, not finding it, though there was enough light coming from outside. She clutched the duvet, gagged a little, swallowed down what had risen. She looked for her slippers, found them at the side of the bed. They hadn't moved at all, not an inch. She turned them over, shook them, wiped her hand through them to dis-lodge the glass that had collected there. A stupid thing to have done. Afterward there'd been splinters and infections in her fingers and feet.

But it couldn't have taken more than a few seconds, get-ting the slippers, because when she stumbled out into the passage, Ross was just leaving his room, wearing only his underwear, the hair on his stomach and chest startling her. "What's happening?" she'd said, as he moved away from her, going toward the front of the house.

He stopped in the open doorway. "Fuck."

She pushed past him onto the front step. The garage was half blown away, small flames on the wrecked walls, in the driveway, and on the lawn. Dark piles lay all around. Paul was already outside, was kneeling beside one of them. "What's happened?" she called.

He looked up, his body moving enough that she could make it out now, could see that it was Deidre in front of him, lying stretched out on the ground like she was already dead. "Call an ambulance," he said. "Hurry!"

She turned, almost fell, had to catch hold of the doorframe, the sickness coming up again and filling her mouth. She raised her head, saw Ross leaving his room, dressed now in jeans and a hoodie, a baseball cap, a backpack in his hand.

"What are you doing?"

"I have to go now, Ma."

"What do you mean? Go where? It's the middle of the night."

"Sorry, Ma, I have to go. I'll be back when I can, okay? Don't worry about me."

He ran to the kitchen, went out through the back door, leaving it open so that she could see him look around the garden, pull the cap down over his face, throw the back-pack over both shoulders. He made for the wall, the one that separated them from a small wetland. There were no paths, no roads, just mud and reeds twice the height of him. He'd get lost in all of that, get lost and fall and drown in the mud. She tried to follow after him, but wasn't able to move from where she stood, her body willing itself to be seated.

Then someone was behind her, that neighbor with the wide mustache who drove the gray Corolla. He was saying, "Where's the phone? Where's the phone?" She pointed to the hall table, it was right here beside her, right here. She had been coming to make the call, she'd been on her way. She watched him pick up the phone, dial, watched him talk into it, that mustache of his moving with every word. But she heard none of it, only a long cry out on the lawn, a long cry that didn't want to end. And outside somewhere Ross was running, running into a darkness from which there seemed to be no return.

But he had come back. Her boy had come back. Here he was as she opened her eyes. Sitting in the chair as though he had been here all night just like he'd promised he would be.

"Where did you go? I've been worried about you."

"I went to get you some flowers." He pointed at a glass vase on her bedside table, a mixed bouquet in pinks and whites, like the kind they used to sell at the entrance to Pick n Pay before the drought.

"They're so expensive now. Where did you even find them?"

"That's not for you to worry about, Ma. Just enjoy them, that's all you have to do."

She reached out her hand to him. "You have to stay with me. I don't want you leaving again. Stay here."

PART THREE

Deidre

"Miriam, come help me with something quickly."

Miriam put her head out, looked up the corridor to where Deidre stood in her own doorway. "I'm busy now. What is it?"

"I need something from the top of the cupboard."

"Jesus." She looked back into her room, then out again. "But just quickly, hey? Roxy's sleeping."

"Ja, just quickly."

She was barefoot, her skin white and flaky at the heels, her shins dry too. She wore leggings, an oversize T-shirt, and no bra, so that her breasts hung low and she seemed to become aware of them as she walked, crossing her arms, holding them in place. "And?" she said as she entered the room. "What's so important?"

Deidre opened the right-hand side of the cupboard, pointed. "That suitcase at the top."

"Okay." She brought a chair across, climbed onto it with a groan. "This brown one here?"

"Ja, that's it."

"It better not be heavy."

"It isn't. It's just some papers and things."

She dragged it out, let it drop to the floor, then stepped down, groaning again. "You going on holiday or something?"

"Ja, I can't decide between Hawaii or fucking Monte Carlo."

"You don't have to be like that. I thought maybe you're going to Monica."

"Nah, she's always saying I must come, but she doesn't get that it's difficult for me. I mean, she should come here."

"For fuck's sake, Deidre, she's got a baby on the way and a business to run. She can't just drop everything and pop over. You're being selfish."

"It's not like that. You don't understand."

"Well, all I know is that if someone paid for me to get out of this shithole and away from it all for even half an hour, I would go. I would be gone; you don't need to ask me twice."

Deidre sniffed, leaned back on the bed, her head against the wall. "Look, I don't want to talk about it, okay? Let's just drop it."

"Fine."

Miriam went to the window, tried to open the curtains, looked up at the rod where a ring had caught fast and wouldn't budge. "What's this now?" she said quietly, the words coming across to Deidre as soft as a cool hand on her forehead. Deidre turned her face toward her, wanting that touch again, that same gentle hand.

But there was no more, the hoop had shifted, the curtain was open, and, "Well, let me get going," Miriam said.

Deidre sat up, blinked, aware now of the brightness of the room. It caught at her throat, clasped her there, a sudden desperation at this light, this bright and horrifying light. The room had shrunk, the depths and shadows had gone, everything small now, smaller than it ought to be. A place of tired excess. All these things she had kept, had demanded to keep, because of what they meant to her; furniture her father had made, decorations from the old house, and all of them, these things she had said she could not live without, stained where she grabbed at them to grip her way around the room, and now this brightness, so that the stains glared, showing her what she already knew herself to be: a thing of need and desperation.

"Wait," she wanted to say. "Stay with me."

But, "Hey," she said, not even looking at Miriam, staring instead at the fabric of her skirt, "you never said what happened with that inspector. Any luck?"

Miriam stopped at the doorway, mimicked, "We'll see what we can do."

"Ja, we've heard that before." It wasn't enough; Miriam had a foot out the door, was saying, "Okay, let me go." So that Deidre, without meaning to bring that place here and speak of it out loud, said, "They've knocked down the houses. The old neighborhood is all gone now."

Miriam came back, leaned her hip against the counter, her arms crossed once more under her breasts. "Ja, I heard. Alistair wants to go look." She shook her head. "But I'm, like, what for? It's just going to depress us, you know?"

"Ja, I know."

She stood a moment, looking around the room, then went over to where she'd dropped the suitcase. "Where you want this?"

Deidre put a hand out beside her. "Just here is fine."

She put the suitcase down and Deidre waited for her to sit, moving her leg to make space, but she remained standing, then frowned and leaned over the bedside table, pushing the window out as far as it would go. "No, jirre, get some fucking air in here. It stinks."

"What are you talking about? It smells fine. Why you in a bad mood now?"

"I'm not in a bad mood. Listen, I want you to listen to me because I am telling you this as a friend. It stinks in here and you stink too. You can't keep living like this. It's disgusting, okay? I'm going to get some wet wipes and when I come back you need to clean yourself, okay? You can't go on like this, I'm telling you."

She waited for Miriam to leave, felt her lip begin to tremble, and she brought a hand up, covered her mouth, her eyes like blisters. She bit down on the inside of her finger. Here was the desperation once more, black within her, and fierce, and all around her this bright and terrifying doom. But she bit her finger, made the pain shift to that small center until she had bitten the tears out of herself.

Soon she stood up, looked inside her bag, knowing already that there would be no cigarettes. Even so, she was irritated, and she put the bag down with force, watching it fall from the clutter of the bedside table onto the floor, then looked across at the blue light of the microwave clock, checked the time on her cellphone to make sure. Too early. Nowhere nearby would be open yet.

She stood a moment, thought what to do, then returned to the bed and drew the suitcase toward her. The zip stuck when she tried it and she had to bring it forward a few times, pull it back gently, until at last it began to shift. She pushed the lid open, smelled the dryness of forgotten papers, of dark cabinets, of a home dismantled.

Monica's birth certificate was on top. She had not expected that, and the tears returned, though she kept them back, did not let them fall. The paper was small, no more than a scrap. Yet her father had struggled to get it, spending weeks in queues at Home Affairs, telling them what he could about how she'd come to them. They had said he must go through Social Services first. "You can't just pick up a child and take it for yourself." But no, he was adopting her, he said. There was no need for all the rest. A year it took, of nothing and nothing, and then he had grown tired, afraid even. He withdrew some money from his investments and simply paid a man he'd come to know at the department to make it happen. A lot of trouble for a piece of paper to say that she was theirs. And here it was. She was about to take a photo of it, send a message asking if Monica didn't need it, but then Miriam was back, carrying a still-sleeping Roxy, holding out a half-empty pack of wet wipes to Deidre. There was nothing to be done now, nothing but will the tears away once more and say, "For fuck's sake, I washed myself a couple of days ago. I'm not going to do this. You're being annoying."

Miriam shook her head. "No, this is not a discussion. Look at me. You need to clean yourself, every single part of yourself, especially between your legs and in your armpits, okay? And don't forget to brush your teeth. Now, what about this bedding and your clothes? When last did you do any washing?"

"I don't know."

"I'm going to take this stuff off here," she said, pulling at the duvet with one hand. "We can take it to the laundry room. They'll do it for you if you pay. But in the meantime, get started with those wipes. I'm not leaving until you come out clean."

Deidre went into the bathroom. The lightbulb wasn't working, so she left the door ajar, stripped herself bare, and sat on the closed toilet. She leaned her elbows on her thighs, rocked forward, a hand over her brows, a finger at her teeth. A couple of tears fell onto the tile beside her foot, and she had to force herself to sit upright, straighten her shoulders. She put her head back and looked up at the ceiling, made her voice hard. "So, where are those fucking wipes?"

Miriam passed them to her, pointed a finger. "Do it properly." She had already taken the linen from the bed; the bare mattress and pillows marked unevenly with yellow and brown. "We'll have to get these pillows washed as well," she said, then leaned across to the suitcase, picked up some of the photos inside. "Hey, what's this stuff?"

Deidre watched for a moment, watched her going through the photos, heard her saying things like "Oh, you were a cute little girl." And "Look at your mom here. I never saw her like this. So smart, hey." She had a wad of wipes in her hand, had passed it over her arms, her breasts, but she went no further now, let the wipes fall. "Don't touch that stuff," she wanted to say. "It's not yours. Don't fucking touch it."

But she remembered the hand fixing the curtain, that cool hand, and she said nothing. Once again, she willed the tears away, tired of the need for it; all these tears that came at her, came at her, wouldn't let her be. She grabbed some more wipes, began on her face and neck, down to her armpits, focused on that, on the fresh smell that was meant to bring comfort.

Then, "Who's this hottie?" Miriam said.

"Who?"

"This one." She held up a photo. A studio portrait of a young man, seventeen, eighteen, in army uniform, his gaze a little off to the right.

"Oh God, I'd forgotten about that one. It used to be in our lounge. It's my mom's baby brother, my uncle Rossouw."

"He's hot."

"I don't know. I mean, I never even met him. He died before I was born."

She reached across to the sink, found a tube of toothpaste. The lid had been left off long ago, the nozzle now clogged and dry. She squeezed a few times, but nothing came out, so she turned it around, put a corner in her mouth, biting until the plastic gave way and she tasted mint. She used her finger to move the paste around her mouth. Without water it stuck in clumps, burned her tongue. She spat out what she could, said, "Okay, I'm done. Give me some clothes."

"Hold on a second." And Miriam was in her cupboard, muttering to herself, before coming to the bathroom door, passing in a bundle. "There's nothing clean, so these'll have to do." She sat back down on the bed. "How did he die?"

"Huh?"

"Your sexy uncle."

"Oh that. Well, it's sort of like this secret scandal, really."

"Ja?"

"Ja. The thing is, he was like the family god, the perfect specimen and everything. I don't know, that side of the family has always been crazy about their sons. So, after high school he's doing his compulsory service and he's all set to go off and fight in the Border War, and the family's already calling him a hero and he's saving the country, just him on his own. I mean, that's the shit my mom always told us, me and Ross, because he was named after him, right, this hero who gave his life for the country and was killed by some scum up there."

"Jesus."

Deidre came out of the bathroom. "Ja, but the thing is that none of it was even true. My dad told me that Rossouw never even made it to the war. He'd fucked some woman somewhere and got gonorrhea from her, and he was scared shitless about it and what his mom would say, so he drank a bottle of pills and choked to death on his own vomit."

"Wow."

"I know. That was the big fucking hero. The hero of South Africa."

She sat down on the other side of the suitcase, began to go through the photos quickly.

"What you looking for?"

She flipped through a few more until she came to what she wanted. "This," she said.

Miriam craned her neck, tried to see. It was a plot of land with a small house behind a sandy driveway. There was an ancient wreck of a car, without wheels or windows or even a bonnet, and beside it a mirror bush that had been left to grow wild. All around were black rubbish bags, bits of metal, wooden planks, buckets and baskets, old ovens, fabric scraps, broom handles, cardboard boxes gone to pulp, a pile of tins, everything surrounded by knee-high grass.

"You don't recognize it?" said Deidre.

Miriam shook her head.

"It's the house, just after my dad bought the place."

"Really? This is the house in Protea Street?" She took the photo from Deidre.

"Ja, looks bad, hey? It was before he fixed it up. Like, you wouldn't be surprised to find dead bodies in there, right?"

"Geez, ja, it looks terrible. I had no idea. I mean, we only moved there, what, like nine, ten years ago. Not that it was perfect, hey, Deidre. You'd let that place get pretty bad yourself."

"I was alone, I didn't have anyone to help me! Monica had fucked off, my mom was . . . Ah, it doesn't matter now. It's gone. And you're right not to go look. It's fucking depressing."

Miriam put the photo back in the suitcase, shifted Roxy. "What, you went? Who took you?"

"Police."

"The police? Jesus, Deidre. The fucking police? Why?"

"Just some bullshit, don't worry about it."

"You know what, I won't worry about it. You can have your little secret." She stood up, moved toward the door. "Listen, I'm going to feed Roxy. I'll come back later and pick up the stuff for washing, so look around and see what else there is, okay?"

"Ja, okay."

She turned back to the suitcase, picked up the photos again. There was another of the original property, taken from the back of the house, showing trees: guava, fig, and hibiscus; broken concrete slabs in the sand; a washing line strung between two slanting poles. Behind them ran a wooden fence, repaired in places with corrugated iron and a variety of slats and scrap wood. In one section the fence had collapsed entirely, showing through to tall reeds from the wetland beyond.

He had torn it all down, put up a concrete wall, a new washing line on brick-paved ground. He put in flower beds, a rose garden, slate stone paths, and a lawn. In front, he clipped the mirror bush, tarred over the driveway, built a garage, cleared a spot for a birdbath, erected a trellis for jasmine. The house had also come down in stages, been built again, extended, with three bedrooms, two bathrooms, a bigger kitchen that could fit a table and chairs.

He had kept only the trees, pruning them back until

they were little more than stumps. Her mother often spoke of that, bringing it up during meals, something for them to laugh over when there was nothing else to say. "He cut them so short that I thought they'd all die," she'd say. "I almost divorced him when I saw what he'd done. Really, I thought they'd never grow again." But by the time Deidre was a girl, with her list of chores, they were growing thick, dropping endless leaves and dead fruit that she had to rake up on Saturday mornings. Her hand blistering just between the thumb and forefinger, and the rake never working properly, spearing the fruit so that she had to stop, touch the wet rottenness of a fig or guava, remove it before she could go on. Sometimes, if she was on her own, she'd fling them up at Ross's birdhouses, try to get them into the holes.

Once, watching a fig split and collapse against a tree, her father called her name. She'd had another in her hand, ready to throw, but let it drop, said, "Sorry." She had forgotten he was there, at the back fence, digging out wide flower beds for her mother, who'd gone to the nursery in Kenilworth to buy plants.

"Come here," he said, and she slouched across the lawn to where he was kneeling in the dirt. He wore a floppy hat, had a thick layer of zinc sunscreen smeared over his nose.

She said again, "Sorry, Daddy," looking down at him, seeing how pink the back of his neck was. He'd forgotten to put anything there, and the sun had been on it, forming a clear line above the collar of an old work shirt that he used now for gardening and painting. He stood up, said, "No, no. Look here," holding out a dark object. "Look what I found."

She thought at first that it was pottery, some ancient thing, black with dirt from being underground so long. But he brought it closer, and she saw that it was a snouted skull with large canines. "What is that?" she said, taking it from him. It was lighter than she'd thought it would be. Gritty, too, the bone almost crumbling in places so that it was uncomfortable to hold.

"I think it's a dog. There's a lot more bones here, but I made such a mess of it while I was digging, so they're all over the place now. Do you want to help me look for them?"

She nodded, knelt down, placing the skull on the grass beside her.

"Let's do it with our hands, okay?" he said. "That way we can be more careful."

She put her hands into the damp black soil, could feel the nuggets of bone easily, those fragments of spine and rib coming to her as though they were floating, set in motion by a dark ebb and flow, raising them up, bringing them forward. She placed her finds next to the skull, watched her dad crawling on his knees, his trousers black and green from the soil and wet grass.

"Look how clean they are," he said, holding up a rib. "There's nothing left on them, no meat, nothing. Just the bone."

"Is it from the olden days?"

He shook his head. "No. It was probably a pet and people buried it here when it died."

"The family before us?"

"That's right."

After a while they began to assemble the skeleton, laying it flat on the grass. The skull first, then the legs. She put the hind ones in the front by mistake, made it look strange, sloping backward. She went to move them, but her dad laughed, said they should turn it into a game, design the skeletons of made-up animals. He created a type of octopus; the skull surrounded by legs from different lengths of bone. Then a snakelike creature with a long spine and no legs. When it was her turn, she propped the skull on two of the larger bones which she had stuck vertically into the ground. "Imagine it trying to walk like this," she said, making the head wag, laughing.

All these years and she hadn't ever thought of that dog. Had never thought of it apart from once. When she was in the hospital, maybe a week after the explosion, and she had been drugged, sick with pain and shock. Pregnant too, had to hear them tell her father, had to see his face at the news. And here they were again, telling her the leg couldn't be saved, they'd tried, but there was nothing more to be done, this was the last option. They'd allowed him to sit on the bed next to her, and he'd put his arm around her, let her cry. She'd said—it had come from nothing, nothing at all, no sensible place, "Will it be like the dog?"

He moved the hair from her forehead, gave her a kiss,

said, "Yes, of course," though he'd not known what she was talking about, didn't understand that she was asking what would happen to the bone. Would it be buried like the dog had been? Buried somewhere dark and far away, where one day children would dig it up, make it move in new and horrifying ways.

In the afternoon Miriam brought back the washing, still warm, smelling clean. "They said they'd send the bill. It's probably going to be pretty expensive because there was so much of it, and they had to use the dryers, especially for the duvet and stuff, but look at them now." She held up the pillows. "Stained and ugly, but at least they're not dirty anymore, right?"

She dusted the bare mattress with bicarb, rubbing it in a little, turned the mattress over, did the same on the other side. "Let's just give that a minute to do its job," she said, then went to the cupboard, sorting through the mess, making a pile of old receipts, empty water bottles, other bits of rubbish. Deidre sat in the chair, watching as Miriam wiped out the shelves with her hand and organized the clean, folded clothes onto them.

"This is something you can do by yourself, you know.

You have the time and you definitely don't need help to keep your cupboards tidy. Anyone can do it."

"I know, it's just, it's this place. I hate it, it doesn't feel like home to me, so why should I keep it tidy?"

"Don't talk rubbish. It's not only here. Things were just as bad at the old house, that place was terrible, the way you lived. You never cleaned there either. You're too lazy."

But it had been too difficult on her own, after her dad died, after Monica left. Dishes stayed dirty, scattered throughout the rooms, clothes lay where they fell. Long clumps of dust dragged through the house, most of them accumulating at the far end of the passage, near the kitchen. Outside, the grass grew long, then withered in the drought. The hydrangeas and roses died. Figs and guavas rotted on the ground, bringing flies and rats. When the lawyer had come about the house, he'd looked around, seen how it was, and went to call Social Services, asked for their help. An inspector came next, going through the rooms with the lawyer, saying quietly to him, "Classic case of neglect."

"That's right," she'd wanted to say from where she'd been following behind them. "I've been neglected."

Still, the shame as they led her into her mother's bedroom later, to "show you her condition," to explain why she had to be removed as soon as possible. As though she hadn't already known. As though she hadn't been living in this waste and dirt with her for years. "Nobody helps me," she'd said.

She turned away from Miriam. "Don't start with that again."

"I'm just saying you can be cleaner and tidier. Like, do your bedding once a month instead of once a year. This place has a good water recycling system for washing, so it's possible. And then just do little bits in the week, like underwear and small things so that you can stay on top of it. I mean, it's not easy, the way things are with the drought, but it's not impossible." She went to the bed, struggled with the corners of the fitted sheet, then put the duvet in its cover, spread it out, got the pillows into their pillowcases. "There you go, good as new."

Deidre stood up from the chair, hopped across, flopped onto the bed. "Ah, that's nice."

"You see."

She pushed her head back into the soft pillows, said, "Hey, so what you doing now? Can you take me to Checkers?"

Miriam put her hand to her face, wiped her forehead. "Seriously? You're asking me to take you to Checkers after I spent the whole day doing shit for you? You always have to push it, Deidre, you always have to have something more."

"Look, don't worry if you can't take me. I was just asking because I don't have anything to eat. But it's fine, I can walk or something."

"Jesus, okay. Okay, I'll take you. You don't have to guilt-trip me. Just give me a minute to get Roxy ready and to change. I'm covered in dirt."

She picked up the pile of trash she'd taken from the cupboard, went to put it in the bin under the sink, pulled up her nose at the smell. She pressed the papers and bottles into it, drew the bag closed, knotted it. She looked up, pointed a finger. "You better have your own money, cause I'm not paying for you this time. I'll take you, but I'm not paying. Enough is enough."

"Ja, relax, man. I've got plenty. Monica sent me some last night. Listen here." She took her phone from the bed-side table, played a voice note: "Hi, Mom. I'm going to call you tomorrow, but I just wanted to say quickly that I put more money in your account like you asked. They said it would transfer immediately, so you don't have to worry about waiting for it, okay? And remember that it's for food and other essentials, like water. It's not for takeaways and booze, okay? I hope you're listening to me. *Buy yourself some water.* Okay, we'll speak later. Love you, bye."

Deidre laughed. "That girl. She hasn't even had the baby yet and look at her, behaving like a mother already."

"But why's she sending you money anyway? Did you already use up your disability?"

Deidre shrugged.

"Just be ready in five minutes, okay. I have my own life too, you know."

She waited while Miriam strapped Roxy into the car seat, then lowered herself into the passenger seat before jumping up, wiping a hand across the back of her skirt and thighs. "Ah shit, it's wet."

"Oh sorry, I forgot. My mom gave me some water this morning and the lid wasn't screwed on properly so it leaked everywhere. I lost, like, half the bottle." She leaned past Roxy to the other side of the backseat, where there was a stack of reusable shopping bags. She took a baby blanket from beneath the pile, folded it over and placed it on the passenger seat. "There you go. Better than nothing."

Deidre sat down again, said, "Fuck," at the dampness coming through, then handed the crutches to Miriam. She put them in the boot, got into the driver's seat, turned the key, the engine sputtering, sputtering until it took to life.

"You need a new car," said Deidre. "This one's getting too old now."

"You want to walk to Checkers? I can stop right now. It's no problem."

"Relax, I was just saying."

Miriam drove slowly to the exit, waited while Winston lifted the boom for them.

Deidre stuck her head out the window. "Hey, what's going on? Why you doing this by hand?"

He pointed at his wrist, though he wasn't wearing a watch. "Loadshedding just started."

"Oh, ja, shit. I forgot."

"Hopefully they've fixed the generator at Checkers by now," said Miriam, and Winston shook his head, said, "Good luck."

They passed the school, a few pupils waiting outside to be picked up, some of them standing alone, looking at their phones, others in pairs or more, talking. Behind them the graffiti still remained on the wall, a little faded from the scrubbing, but clear enough. Then there was laughter, a boy stealing the scarf from one of the girls, running away with it, looking over his shoulder as she chased him. She caught him, punched his arm, laughed with him, her hair falling in her eyes.

Beyond them, from a side street, came Rodney with Queenie. He was pushing a trolley full of empty bottles and bits of cardboard, talking to himself as he often did. Miriam gave a little honk of the horn, waved as he looked up. Deidre waved too, smiled. He waved back, shouted something they couldn't hear, and then they were past the block, at the next one with its four stories and reflective windows: the frail care center, owned by the same man who had built the place where they lived. Deidre didn't turn her head but could see from the corner of her eye how a man in the same uniform as Winston's was lifting a boom, allowing a truck in through the delivery entrance. She'd never been inside, could guess what it looked like though.

Beside her Miriam said, "I'll pick up a couple of tins of food for him. He's not looking so good today."

"Who?"

"Rodney."

At the four-way stop they waited for two middle-aged women to cross, wearing matching T-shirts in party colors. One was carrying a ladder, the other had a number of posters under her arm. They'd already put up a few of them on the lampposts. The woman with the ladder smiled across at them, calling, "Don't forget to vote, ladies. Help us to help you."

Miriam looked away, turned, drove on for a minute before saying, "Fucking cheek, hey? Expecting we'll vote for them. Not a chance! I voted for them last time and where did it get us? All those promises and look where we are today, worse off than we were before. It's a fucking cheek."

Deidre scratched her neck, said, "Ja, it's bullshit."

"So, do you have any idea who you'll be voting for? I mean, you don't have to tell me, I'm just wondering cause me and Alistair, we're stuck. We don't trust any of them, so at this point it's like who do we think will fuck us over the least, you know? It's keeping me awake at night, I can tell you. Really, I'm sick about it, just sick."

"Ja, well, for me it's easy cause I'm not voting."

"No? Like in protest or something?"

"No, nothing like that. I'm just not voting. I never have, I'm not even registered to vote."

Miriam looked across at her. "What the fuck, Deidre? You never voted, like never ever?"

"Don't shout at me. Jesus. No, I have never voted. Why's it such a big deal? I mean, why do you even care?"

"I just don't understand it, like how's it even possible?"

She shrugged, scratched her neck again. "Well, I guess I could've voted in 'ninety-four because I was eighteen, but no one ever talked to me about it or told me to register or anything like that, and my parents weren't really political people. They didn't vote either, so it's just not something we did in our house. And then, you know, my leg happened, so I couldn't have voted anyway . . ."

"Okay, you lost your leg, but that was a long time ago. What about afterward, all the other elections since then?"

"I don't know what you want me to say, it just wasn't a big deal in our family, all that politics and shit. It didn't affect us, you know."

"It didn't affect you? Are you serious?"

Deidre put her hands up in front of her. "Listen, it's different for you. You're Colored so voting actually means something to you and your people because you were kept from it for all those years. So for you voting is like really meaningful, it has an actual reason."

"I can't believe what you're saying. Can you even hear yourself? Voting isn't just for Coloreds or Blacks. It has a reason for everyone."

She shrugged, pushing out her lower lip. "I just never saw the point for me. The government doesn't care about me, so why waste my time on it?"

"Seriously?" The car swerved a little, but Miriam righted it at once, kept her eyes on the road. "You fucking live off a fucking disability grant. You don't think that involves the government caring about you?"

"Just relax, you're getting too upset. I don't vote, I never have, that's all there is to it. Isn't that my choice?"

Miriam shook her head, chewed the insides of her cheeks. "You know what, Deidre, you're really something else. Every time I think I've seen the worst of you, you come out with something even more terrible. Every single time, no matter what. Are you trying to be unpleasant, tell me? Is that your plan, to be unpleasant and make everyone dislike you? I really want to know."

Deidre looked down into her lap. "No. It's just the way I am."

Miriam turned in at the parking lot, the car bumping over the roots of the massive pines that had long since pushed up out of the tar. She shook her head at the car guards who were pointing out empty bays to her, drove instead to the handicapped spot right outside the entrance. She got out, went to the boot, picked up the crutches and handed them to Deidre. "Listen, I don't think I'm going in with you."

"Come on, don't be like this. I'm sorry, okay? I'll vote next time. You can take me to register and tell me who to vote for. I don't care."

"Oh my God, Deidre, that's not the point."

"So what is the point then, huh? Because I don't know what you're getting so fucking upset about. Is it because I called you Colored?"

Miriam took a deep breath, looked around at the people passing by, spoke quietly. "We've known each other a long time, from back in Protea Street, and, okay, we weren't exactly friends, but we knew each other. I used to see you on your own, and the neighbors told me all about what had happened to your leg and about your brother, and about the situation with your mother too. And I said to Alistair, 'That lady's lost, she needs our help.' And I did help you out a bit, didn't I? Not a lot, but a few times, right?"

"Ja, so?"

"So, then the government comes and kicks us out and here we are in our little rooms, living next to each other, and it's been more than two years now, more than two years of you coming to me every fucking day with your demands. It doesn't matter to you if I'm sick or busy or pregnant or breastfeeding. No, it's just 'Do this for me, do that for me, help me, help me, I'm a fucking cripple and I can't do any-thing for myself.'"

"I am a fucking cripple."

"No, what you are is the most selfish person I've ever met. You don't care about anyone except yourself. Do you know who visits your mother, do you know who goes every week to check if she has everything she needs, if she's okay? I don't even fucking know the woman and she has no clue who I am, but I go to her and I take baby powder and paja-mas and socks and chocolates so that she has something nice once in a while. When have you gone, huh? She lives across the fucking street and you can't walk a hundred meters to see your own fucking mother."

"You know that's not how it is. It's complicated with me and her."

"Everything's complicated with you. Everyone else's life is a piece of cake, a fucking walk in the park, right? No one has problems except you. You're the only one who is having a shit time. You're the only one who needs help."

"So, you help me out once in a while, what's the big deal? That's what friends do."

"That's right. Friends do help each other, Deidre, but we're not friends. In all the time I've known you, you've never done anything for me, never even said a fucking nice word to me. Never said a thing about anything or anyone if it isn't to complain. You're a selfish, miserable bitch and I'm sick of you. I'm done. I've had enough."

"Just—"

She turned away, got in the car. "I've got things to do. I'll be back to pick you up at five."

Deidre watched Miriam start the car, heard the engine spit, spit, felt the sudden lift as it caught. Then Miriam was pulling away, was leaving, and Deidre stood alone, her eyes once more blistered. She thought of earlier, of the cool hand on her brow, strained to feel the curtain's movement, the whisper of the metal ring shifting along the rod, but somewhere behind the building the supermarket's generator was running, and the relentless gray moan of it made its way inside her, made her swallow what had been gentle, made her say "Fuck you" out loud. Fuck you to Miriam, and fuck you to that other thing, that invisible thing that came at her from all directions. Every day coming at her, from the sky, from the horizon, from mountains and streets and worn-out pavements where grass never grew, from every corner, this thing that was always watching her, that never took its eyes off her. That saw what she was and punished her for it.

The shop was full, bright enough, the tills functioning. She moved awkwardly, knocking people with her crutches, shoving the trolley into them. Fucking Miriam, fucking Miriam, who knew she couldn't do this on her own, knew it, and had made her come in by herself. She didn't understand, didn't know what it was like; she had both her legs, had an education, a husband, a mother who saved water for her. She didn't know what it meant to be alone, to be crippled and alone.

"Excuse me," she called, then again, until people began to turn around, clear a path. She did not thank them, let them look at her, shake their heads, mutter under their breaths. She went first toward the fruit and vegetables, knowing the displays would be close to empty. A scattering of tiny naartjies, each no bigger than a baby's fist. Mesh bags of ill-formed onions and potatoes. Apples imported from Australia. She picked up a couple, put them back; too expensive. Then made for the wire rack that was usually wheeled out at around this time with food items about to expire, all of them marked down. A few people had arrived before her, were already picking through the lot. She pushed forward, grabbed three donuts on a Styrofoam plate covered in plastic wrap, a serving of potato salad, two lemon-and-poppyseed muffins, yesterday's ciabatta.

At the cold meats fridge, she took a budget pack of Viennas, the weight of it clammy and unwieldy, so that it slipped from her hand, fell into the trolley with a wet smack. From the aisles she took cheese spread, Marmite, tea bags, a big value box of cream crackers, four long-life milks, five tins of spaghetti in tomato sauce, three 2-liter Cokes. But there were other things she looked at, things she picked up and put back: basil pesto, chocolate-covered almonds, tinned salmon, blueberry-flavored sparkling water. In the toiletries aisle she stood with a bottle of shampoo, put it in the trolley, took it out again. She added a bar of soap instead, roll-on deodorant, mouthwash, and a cheap bottle of poppy-scented body spray. She took another bottle from the shelf, removed the cap, sprayed it across her chest, up and down her arms. The cap dropped out of her hand, rolled under the shelves. She put the bottle back, walked on.

At the far end of the supermarket was a large display of wine, a new import from Chile, the South African industry no longer producing as it had. The display jutted out, made it impossible for her to get around it. She stopped a boy in his school uniform, said, "Hey, do me a favor quickly."

"Yes, of course, ma'am."

She pointed at the wine aisle. "I want two 5-liter boxes."

He blushed, glanced at the black-and-white sign that warned alcohol was sold only to those who were eighteen years or older. "I don't know."

"Look, don't worry," she said, seeing the prefect badge on his lapel, a badge for academic excellence beneath it. "I'm not asking you to buy it for me."

He looked at her leg, her trolley, the sign, said at last, "What is the name of the wine you'd like?"

"God, I don't know. It's just the no-name-brand one, Red Blend or something. The box is black and red with a wineglass on it."

He went around the corner, came back a moment later, holding up a five-liter box. "Is this correct?"

"Ja, but I want two."

He ducked back, got another, placed them in the trolley, asking if there was anything else he could do to help.

"Ja, just push this to that till over there."

The boy looked at the trolley. "Um, ma'am, that is an express till and I think you might have more than ten items here."

"Jesus," she said. "I'll just do it myself, like I do everything else in my fucking life."

There were two people ahead of her in the queue, and already three behind her. When it was her turn, she called to a packer, a man with Down syndrome, who was standing at the neighboring till. "Hey, Devon, come help me over here."

He came across, pulled the trolley through for her and began to unload the items.

"I can do that," she said when he'd almost finished. "You go get some cigarettes for me. You still know the kind I like?"

He nodded. "One?"

She looked at him, the cashier, the lady behind her in the queue. "You know what, today I'm going to treat myself. Bring me a whole fucking carton. That's ten packs, right?"

"I'll check."

She watched him cross to the cigarette counter, speak to

the lady there, get the carton, carefully count the packs inside, bring them back. "It's ten," he said, handing them to the cashier and beginning to place the swiped items into a recyclable plastic bag.

"Hold on, I brought my own today. I'm not paying for that." She pointed at her backpack, which was still in the trolley. "There's a few bags inside there." Then, as the cashier swiped the wine, she said to Devon, "Put one of those inside the backpack, and zip it up again, okay?"

After paying, she got him to push the trolley outside to a bench near the handicapped parking bay, said, "Thanks, man, you're a good guy." She thought she ought to give him a tip and she ripped open the carton of cigarettes, fumbled with a pack. "Uh, you want a smoke?"

"No, thank you. Have a nice day."

"Ja, you too."

She lit one for herself, checked the time on her phone. Ten to five. Miriam would probably be late, make her wait, just to be a fucking bitch. She looked through her purchases, was about to reach for a pink-frosted donut when she changed her mind, got up, walked back to the entrance. A woman had a kiosk there, was frying onions, greasy sausages on a hot plate, making boerewors rolls. "You take cards?"

"Yes, lady."

"Okay," she held out her card, "I'll take one." After she'd paid, she said, "Can you bring it to that bench over there, it's difficult for me with these things."

The woman nodded, pushed the onions around on the hot plate. "One minute, dear."

Deidre sat, looked out across the parking lot. It was empty at the further end, with nothing but the cracked tar, the crumbling mounds where tree roots pushed through. Yet beyond, just across from the exit, was a long green avenue. Two men were walking with a young girl as she rode a bike, walking and laughing, the girl laughing with them. And then they had gone, all three of them disappearing through a gate, as though entering some verdant promise, untouched by drought, while in the parking lot plastic bags rose, settled, rose again. Pigeons landed, stood alone, flew off, and no other thing moved amidst the barren leavings.

The woman brought the boerewors roll over, and Deidre blew on the hot sausage, bit into it, tasting the fatty warmth of the meat and onions. She bit again, chewed twice, took another bite. If there was time, she would buy one more, take it home for supper.

"Deidre? Yes, I thought it was you."

She looked up, wiping a hand across her mouth. "Oh, hi, Mrs. Schilling."

"You must excuse the state of me, I've just been to the gym." She pulled at the T-shirt she was wearing. "You have to take care of your health at my age. But tell me, how are you? How's your mother? I haven't seen either of you in ages."

"Fine."

"That's good. I did wonder because a friend of mine, she has a sister in Oak View. She broke her hip a while ago and she's just not recovering. She can't walk or anything. It's very frustrating, but then you know all about that."

"Right."

"She says your mom isn't doing too well. Her mind, you know, and I said to her, 'Oh, Trudy's mind hasn't been well for thirty years or more.' But apparently now it's worse."

Deidre stopped chewing, put the boerewors roll down on her lap.

"Well, it's a shame. I always said it would end badly when they didn't catch your brother. I know it's not my place to say, but he should have been brought back and forced to see what he had done to her. But that's just my opinion, for what it's worth. Anyway, at least she has you, and you're right across the road in Oak Bend, aren't you?"

She nodded.

"Yes, I think it was Lucy Pienaar who told me that. Because we were all so worried when we heard about the house being taken. We didn't know what would happen to her, and then we heard where she was and we were glad you were close by because, really, we did worry."

"Right," she said, struggling to speak with what was still in her mouth, "you were worried. But not enough to ever visit either of us for all those years, and not enough to visit now."

Mrs. Schilling blinked, opened her mouth, looked

around to see if anyone had heard. "Well, Deidre, I can see that you haven't changed. Do give your mother my love when you see her."

She felt the tears again, and worse, that old nausea in her throat, a wound that would not heal. All of her hot and brittle now, and across the way that peaceful green avenue which she could not enter, so that she was left sitting here, the words hard within her, "What about me? What the fuck about me?"

Trudy

She opened her eyes. Saw him sitting there with a cigarette between his lips.

"No smoking," she said. "They'll make you leave."

He took the cigarette from his mouth, held it out for her to see. "It's not lit. Just a bad habit."

"You didn't smoke before."

"There's a lot of things I didn't do before, Ma. It's been a long time, you know."

"I know."

Her throat was dry, always so dry, and she coughed a little. He brought the cup over from the bedside table, held the straw to her mouth as she drank. She could see the stains on his fingers, smell fresh smoke on them and on his clothes. He'd been outside while she was asleep, had gone somewhere outside, into the street, away from the building, and he'd smoked. She looked at him in his two-tone shirt, his hair too long at the back. Someone might have seen him. Someone from the old neighborhood, someone who had known him before might have driven past, recognized him, called the police. She pushed the cup away, began to say that he shouldn't leave the room, that he should stay here with her where he'd be safe, knowing as she opened her mouth how she must sound, knowing that it wasn't possible to keep him beside her at all times. He had to eat, he had to wash and sleep, he had to work. He couldn't do that in this room, not day after day, not without being noticed. Someone might come in at any time, demand to know who he was, to see some kind of identification. What then? What use would she be, lying here without strength to do more than reach across and hold his stained hand?

"Where are you living?" she said. "Is it safe? Are you safe?"

But he didn't answer, said instead, "Grandpa smoked a pipe, didn't he?"

She hadn't expected that, had to think about it for a moment. "That's right. A pipe. Do you remember him? You were so small when he died."

"I remember us going out to their place. Where was it, Bellville?"

"Durbanville."

"Durbanville. I remember the pond with the ducks. And I remember going into a room at the end of a dark passage with wooden floors. It didn't have a door, just a curtain. I went inside and there was a bed and there was something inside the bed under blankets. I didn't know what it was. I went up to it and stood next to it."

"What happened?"

"Nothing. The thing inside the bed moved and I could see a head, and then his eyes opened and his face was white and strange, like, I don't know. He looked at me and he said, it was almost a whisper, he said, 'Little boy.' I was afraid and I ran from the room."

She nodded. "That's how he was in the end. He'd been a heavy drinker. All my life, he drank."

In the corridor there were footsteps, a nurse walking quickly and evenly, speaking sharply to someone. There came the mumble of a reply, then more sharp words, and the footsteps moved on.

Trudy looked across at Ross. "Did he say anything else to you?"

"Who?"

"My father."

He shook his head. "I don't think so. Just that one thing—'Little boy'—that's it."

He stood up, went to the window, separated two slats of the blind with his fingers. He peered out into the glare. "I don't remember seeing him again after that day. I think he must have died soon afterward."

She could still smell the tobacco on him, even from the bed. "Your father sometimes smoked when he was stressed.

Deidre too," she said. "And she drinks. She thinks I don't know about it, but I know."

He turned around. "She's okay though, isn't she? I mean, she recovered from the accident?"

"You'll have a lot to do at the house. She hasn't taken care of it."

He removed his fingers from the blind, shutting out the light. She blinked a few times. "Have you been there yet?"

"No, not yet."

"You need to talk to Deidre. That house is your inheritance. You're the eldest, the only son. It's owed to you."

"Yes, Ma."

"But you won't make her leave?"

"I'll talk to her about it. Don't worry. I'll sort it out."

She leaned back against her pillow. "Good. You're a good boy." Then, sitting up again, "It needs work. It needs a lot of repairs. It was starting to fall down around us. The walls—"

He placed a hand on her shoulder, gentled her back down. "Don't worry, Ma. I'll fix it. I'll fix everything. You're tired now; close your eyes for a bit."

She began to speak again, but he squeezed her shoulder, said, "Just rest for a little while now."

She wanted to tell him about the cracks. How they'd become steadily worse after the accident. New ones formed too, running along the ceilings and walls, extending through the months and years until no room was free from them. Each had its clutch of fine arms and fingers that reached out and out and out. Later, when she was bedbound, staring up at that, not knowing whether Deidre was in the house or whether she was off somewhere, doing God knows what. Calling for her and then straining to hear if she answered, listening for the sighing and mumbling, the crutches coming toward her, waiting for her to arrive, then saying to her, "It's going to come down on top of us."

They had painted the house one year, over the Easter weekend. The kitchen had those tiles that went halfway up the wall, beige ones with a brown-leaf pattern, long since out of date. Ross had bordered them with masking tape, so precise always, and had painted the walls and ceiling, doing it easily because he was tall. All of it without a word of complaint, just getting on and doing it, and going afterward with a wet rag and wiping off the tiles where paint had slipped under the tape. Then she'd come in from Pick n Pay the following Saturday afternoon with some groceries and a box of marshmallow Easter eggs that had been on sale. She'd placed the shopping bags on the counter and looked up at the wall, noticing a fine, short crack in the middle where the tiles met the plaster.

She heard footsteps behind her and turned, thinking it was Paul, wanting to point it out to him and ask whether it was normal for it to be there. But it was Deidre, coming in from outside, where she'd been raking leaves.

"Look at that crack already," she said.

"Ja, there's one in the lounge too." Then, "I'm starving. What's there to eat?"

"You can have an orange or a slice of toast with some jam." She looked at her watch. "But not too much, it's two hours until suppertime."

Deidre moved around as Trudy packed away the shopping. She took a slice from the old loaf in the bread bin, put it in the toaster. She got a plate and a knife, went to the fridge for jam and margarine.

Trudy said, "Excuse me a second," and leaned past her to place a liter of milk and a two-liter bottle of Coke in the fridge door.

"Oh cool, Coke," said Deidre, reaching for it and putting it down on the counter beside her plate. She took a few steps, fetched a glass from the cupboard above the sink.

Trudy said, "What are you doing?"

"What do you mean?"

"That Coke's for your brother. You know that."

"I thought because I'd done the leaves . . ."

"Deidre, I've been asking you all day to do those leaves. And you chose to spend your time in front of the TV. You've only just done them, you left it to the last minute, and you probably did it badly. Meanwhile your brother is working all hours of the day and night, always working. He needs the Coke to give him energy. But you're just going to go sit in front of the TV again. You don't need energy to do that, do you?"

Deidre didn't say a word. She put the Coke back, filled her glass at the tap. She removed the toast from the toaster, spread margarine on it, then left the room. Trudy could hear her going into the lounge and switching on the TV.

Later, after supper, Trudy was sitting on one of the couches, doing as her mom had always done, making sure everyone in the house had their own monogrammed handkerchief to keep with them at all times. It was a tradition of sorts, handed down across several generations, from mother to daughter. It gave Trudy something to do during the long evenings before bed while Ross was busy in the garage and Paul was dozing in the armchair. Deidre lay spread across the other couch, watching a police drama. A Saturday night, but she hadn't asked to go out and spend time with her friends, had simply sat through supper, picking at her food, then showered and put on her pajamas before going to the couch with a blanket and pillow, changing between the four channels until she'd found something she liked.

"Deidre, love," Trudy said, "come sit here next to me for a bit. See what I'm making for you this time. I thought I'd add a strawberry border. I can show you how to do it then you can make these for your children one day too."

Deidre sighed, but didn't move from the couch, only raised her head a little. "Ma, I don't need to know how to do that. I never use those things. They're gross."

She looked at her, that angry face, always frowning, said, "You know, it was the same for me, with Rossouw."

"What?"

"Sometimes it felt like he got everything. But it was because of what he was. He went to the war, you know. He could have been something if he hadn't died. He had it in him to be something really special."

Deidre kept her eyes on the TV. "I could be something. I don't think a bit of Coke will make a difference either way to what I become."

"Of course you can be something. No one ever said you couldn't. It's just that there are people, like your brother, like my brother. They can be just a little bit more. Look at the way Ross works and works and works. Look at what he does. And you can't say you really try, can you?"

Deidre rolled her eyes. "Okay, Ma. Thanks."

Above their heads, that crack running along the ceiling, stretching out, touching every part of the house, and all the years to come, marking everything.

She turned from the memory, turned back to Ross and the narrow bed in the murky room. "I'm dying," she said.

"No, Ma. You're not dying. You're getting better. We're going to the house, we're going to fix it and live there. I promise."

PART FOUR

Deidre

She woke to fire, recognized the smell at once without the need to get up and look out of the window, knew that the mountain was burning. Already ash was falling. She could taste it, though she had her back to the window, was lying on her side with her eyes shut, her body in discomfort. Something red and violent was between her legs, something that extended up into her so that it gripped her bladder and stomach. She was careful of moving, afraid to increase the discomfort. Yet it seemed to sharpen of its own accord, until she could no longer ignore it and had to turn over, blink at the sunlight, at the ash on her bedside table. She rose with difficulty and hovered over the mixing bowl, squatting there as the violence worked at her, but nothing came, nothing. Then, a drop. And another. Nothing more.

She looked into the bowl, saw dark liquid touched by blood, the sight of it like a curse. She stood with the doom of it upon her, went to the kitchen. No water, and too late now to collect it from the truck. A quarter of a two-liter bottle of Coke on the counter and she drank that down, the remaining fizz dying on her tongue and then the sweetness afterward, only the sweetness. That made it worse, made the violence caustic, driving her back to the bowl. Again crouching, crouching, and still no more than a drop. Everything inside her decaying now, everything rotting and dead, yet being held jealously in place, so that there could be no release, no aborting this suppuration.

She called for Hussain, waiting at the bottom of the steps.

"Oh, Deidre, it's you," he said, coming to stand in the doorway.

"I need a lighter."

He nodded, began to turn back, then stopped. "I don't know if I should be selling those things anymore. They say all these fires, most of them are because of cigarettes."

"For fuck's sake, Hussain, don't start with that now. Just get me the lighter, okay."

He didn't say anything, went inside.

"Hey," she called, "and bring me, like, I don't know, like one of those half-liter bottles of water. And the machine; I'm paying by card."

She could hear a radio as she waited, the news on the hour. Evacuations already in place at Noordhoek and Red Hill. Road closures at Constantia Nek. She looked up, past the gabled roof, into the distance where the mountain was burning, the sky dark with smoke and debris. Ash on her face, ash on the handles of her crutches. Same as usual, same fucking story over and over, of fire and drought, of the world burning up and shriveling all around.

She glanced up toward Main Road, could make out Bliksem's shape crossing to a bin, looking inside, shaking a bottle, bringing it to his lips. She took out her phone. 8:27. Hours to go still and this violence within her climbing into her throat, with nowhere to take it. She fumbled for a cigarette, put it in her mouth, waited for the lighter, remembering then the box of wine next to her bed, the mug waiting beside it. She could feel her hand on the mug, could smell the wine pouring into it. "Come the fuck on," she called to the open door, and "Come on" again as Hussain made his way down the stairs to her. She grabbed the water, drank it down like a penance, then took the lighter, lit her cigarette, inhaled deeply.

Winston was standing on the grass-covered traffic island between the entrance and exit lanes of Oak Bend, looking up at the sky, watching two helicopters taking turns dropping water bombs.

"Mornings," he said, dipping his head in the direction of the fire. "I heard there's going to be rain. It's on the way today or tomorrow and it's going to stop this thing in no time."

"Not this shit again, man, seriously, who's telling you this rubbish?" Then, "Oh, listen," she put her hand in her purse, handed him a half-empty pack of cigarettes. "Here, take it. It's all I got, but take it," though she had six more in her room.

"Now I know the rain is coming for sure!" he said, shaking his head with a laugh. "The day Deidre pays back a debt, even just a little bit, that's a day for miracles."

"Shut up, man. Don't make jokes. I don't need jokes."

"Ah, everybody needs jokes."

"Nah, fuck it. I'm not in the mood. I'm telling you, I'm tired of everything. I'm fed up."

A car came from the parking lot and paused at the exit boom. The driver, an old woman she didn't know, with an old man in the passenger seat, waved at them. Winston walked across, bent down, and spoke to the couple for a minute. All three of them laughing, smiling, talking too loudly.

Deidre turned her back to them, looked in her purse for another cigarette, forgetting she had none. She'd get one back from Winston, and she stood waiting, flicking the lighter impatiently, heard the creak of the boom opening, the couple calling, "Bye now, bye-bye."

When they'd gone, he came to stand beside her again, said, "Thanks for the smokes, I didn't—Hey, here's your friend."

She turned around, expecting Miriam, was about to ask for a lift to the pharmacy. But it was Mabombo, pulling up in the handicapped space. "Ah, fuck."

He got out of the car, removing his sunglasses as he shut the door. He nodded at Winston, said, "Good morning," then turned to Deidre and said the same.

"What do you want?"

"Miss van Deventer, I have been trying to call you for a couple of days."

"I told you I don't want to speak to you."

"Ma'am, the fact is that even though you don't want to

speak to us, we very much need to speak to you. We would like you to come and identify a few items, as we mentioned to you previously. Is now a convenient time?"

"No."

"Could you tell me when would be a good time? Maybe this afternoon, or perhaps this evening? It's very important that we have this meeting."

She rolled her eyes. "Jesus, don't you have better things to do? There's a fucking fire. Don't you need to be evacuating people, actually helping people, instead of harassing them?"

"If you consider yourself harassed, ma'am, I'll be happy to let you take it up with Detective Constable Xaba at the station." He turned back to the car, opened the passenger-side door.

"For fuck's sake, fine. Okay, let's go. Let's fucking go."

The car smelled the same as before, was just as neat. The sweets had been replenished and she took a few while Mabombo put the crutches in the back. He got in, turned the ignition, and the radio started playing. It was tuned to Fine Music Radio, a piece that she recognized but didn't know the name of. Beethoven or Bach or someone like that. She made a little sound at it, gave a half smile.

Mabombo looked up at her as he was reversing. "Ma'am, is it bothering you? Should I switch it off?"

She shook her head, leaned forward, drew her ear toward the speaker. Before her the wipers moved through fallen ash. It splintered, softened, made streaks across the glass.

"I can turn the sound up if you like," he said and she shrugged, leaning back again, listening for a few minutes longer before adding, "It's this classical stuff, it reminds me of my daughter. She used to like it when she was at school."

He glanced at her, looked back at the road. "She liked classical music? That isn't something you usually hear about teenagers."

"She'd listen to it when she was studying or doing her homework. She said it helped her concentrate."

"Yes."

The music changed, something slower. In front of her the streaks of ash grew and thinned, grew and thinned.

"Did I tell you she's pregnant?"

He shook his head. "No, you didn't. Congratulations."

"Well, she's playing this stuff for the baby now too. She bought some music specially designed for the womb or something and she plays it right into her belly."

"Ah, yes, I've heard about that. I think it is quite common."

"You know she's black?"

He shifted uncomfortably, changed gear.

"I mean, her skin is black. She looks black. I don't know, how does it work now? Who's black and who isn't?"

Mabombo slowed for a stop sign, came to a halt. "Um, well, I think rules like that ended a long time ago."

"Ja, I suppose you're right."

He turned left, driving slowly, the windscreen thick with smudges.

"I'm just asking," she said, "because sometimes I wonder if maybe she felt a little lost, you know, like not knowing where she came from, who her parents were, or anything like that about her past. And maybe that's why she left, and why she doesn't want to come back, even though she gives other reasons."

"Like what?"

"Well, like she says, listen to this, she says that her whole life she never heard anything except people complaining about the New South Africa, about how the country was going to shit and everything was shit. So she said she made up her mind to leave for a place with a future."

"I see."

"But what I want to know is what did she expect us to do? I mean, of course things were shit and we complained about it. My dad lost his job, I lost my fucking leg." She laughed. "And Ma lost her mind."

"Your mother has had some difficulties?"

"Oh ja, she's totally off her head. It started after the explosion, but I don't know if she even remembers it that way. I mean, she'd look at me sometimes, like look at my leg as though she had no idea how I'd lost it, as if the explosion never happened."

"It must have been difficult for you."

She shrugged, took a couple of sweets from the cup-holder. She held one out to him. "You want?"

He shook his head. "No, thank you."

They drove in silence for a while, Mabombo peering through the windscreen, clicking his tongue. Then, "This isn't working," and he pulled the car to the side of the road, parking with his hazards on. He reached into the cubby-hole for a small bottle of water and then got out, pouring it over the glass. When he got back in, he turned the wipers on again. "Let's hope this works." The smudges darkened at first, but soon two partly clean arcs appeared. "That's better."

She gave a little nod. "Yep."

But he didn't turn back onto the road, stayed where he was. "Um, may I ask . . . your daughter . . . it was a private adoption, wasn't it? You didn't go through an agency or organization or anything like that?"

"What's the problem?"

"No, nothing, nothing. I told you, my wife and I are planning to adopt. Was it . . . Please excuse me, but you adopted her when you were very young, and, well, didn't you want children of your own one day?"

"I wasn't so young, like twenty. It's old enough."

"Yes, of course."

"Anyway, I couldn't have children of my own."

"Oh, I'm sorry to hear that."

"I was pregnant once though," she said, unwrapping another sweet. "It was a long time ago, when I was eighteen. I had this boyfriend, Simon, but my mom didn't like him."

"No? Why not?"

"Normal reasons. He was older than me and he had a motorbike, and he was lower class, you know. Like not good enough in her opinion. But you know how girls are. I thought he was the best thing in the world, and if my mom didn't like him, well, that just made it better."

"Where did you meet him?"

"At that KFC that used to be there in Gabriel Road."

"Oh yes."

"Ja, I was just standing outside with these two girls from school, because we'd been to one of their houses to watch a movie and then afterward we went to the KFC. We were standing outside, waiting for my dad to come pick me up, and Simon came along on this motorbike and started talking to us. Nothing interesting, just like 'Hey, how are you, what you up to?' kind of stuff. I don't know, I just found him sort of nice, I suppose. He had this floppy hair and an earring, which, you know, was pretty sexy back then. And this old leather jacket that was peeling at the shoulders. And we just talked a bit and he gave me a cigarette and offered to take me for a ride, but my dad was coming, so I made a plan to meet him another day. And that's it really, five months of sneaking around."

"Your parents didn't find out about him?"

"Oh ja, they did. They absolutely did, and they said I couldn't see him anymore. So, for a little while I stopped, just to get them off my case, but then I found out I was pregnant, and I wanted to tell him because I had this idea that we could get married and be together."

"So, what happened?"

"This happened." She pointed at her stump.

"You were damaged, internally too?"

She nodded.

"And what about Simon?"

"Never saw him again."

"I'm sorry."

"It's okay, because then Monica came into our lives."

"How? I mean, it doesn't sound like it was your idea. Did your parents organize it? I'm not sure I really understand the situation."

"Ah, it's complicated. I don't want to talk about it." She reached over and turned the volume up, but she could hear only the squealing motion of the windscreen wipers, the fanning out of ash and darkness, and beyond it the oppression of the mountain, the burden of flame and smoke.

He led her into a room with nothing inside it apart from four chairs and a table with a plastic tablecloth that didn't want to hang properly, its edges sticking out toward her. He helped her to sit and said, "I'll be back in a moment. Can I bring you anything?"

"Ja, tea. Six sugars."

She sat chewing on the last of the sweets from the car. She drummed her fingers, looked around. There was a poster about saving energy and remembering to switch off lights. Against the windows were tattered venetian blinds, lopsided, missing slats. Directly above her there was a large, flaking hole. She bent her neck, looked up into it, but couldn't see beyond the blackness of the interior. Her foot caught on linoleum as she shifted, a patch of floor coming loose and lifting with her heel. She shook it off, let it fall, then drummed her fingers again.

He returned, holding a large mug with green and white

horizontal stripes. Under an arm were some plastic ziplock bags.

"Here we are," he said, handing her the mug. It was filled to the top.

"Nice what taxpayer money gets you, huh?" she said, taking a sip. "The rest of us are dying for water, and here you are swimming in it."

Mabombo sat down on the other side of the table, arranging the bags in front of him. "The station has an allotment of water, ma'am, just as everyone in the province does. I made the tea with water from my personal daily allowance. The sugar is mine too."

She put down the mug. "Oh."

He reached for one of the bags. "Shall we begin?"

She looked around at the door. "No Zaba?"

"Detective Constable Xaba will be joining us shortly. In the meantime, could you look at these items and tell me if you recognize any of them?"

She took the bag as he handed it to her. There were several old coins inside, ones that were no longer in circulation. "How do you expect me to know if I recognize these?" He handed her another bag, this one containing a dirt-laden metal toy car. "Nope." The next bag held a table knife. "Ja, okay, you got me. Here's the fucking murder weapon."

Mabombo said nothing, wrote something in his notebook.

"Jesus, I'm joking, you don't need to get so excited. It's just an old knife from the kitchen that my dad used to gar-

den with, like for digging out weeds from between the pav-
ing slabs. It stayed outside; it was always sticking out of a
flowerpot or something. I mean, it's not like it was even
sharp or anything. You couldn't hurt anyone with that. You
can't arrest someone for having a fucking knife like this in
their garden."

He nodded. "And what about this last one?" He held
out the packet to her.

She took it, smoothed the plastic to see better. It was a
small piece of a decorative tile.

"I don't know. Maybe it's from inside the garage. There
were some tiles in there on the wall, I think, but I don't
know. I didn't really go in there. Maybe it's just from the
ground. We were always digging up shit like this. I told you
before, the place was a dump when my dad bought it."

"Yes, ma'am, the investigation—"

"No, I've told you, you're investigating the wrong people, you're looking at the wrong things. Listen, think about
it, that property has been standing empty for two years.
Two fucking years. Some pervert probably used it as a
dumping ground. I mean, did you ever think of that?"

Just then Xaba opened the door, carrying more of the
same ziplock bags with her. She walked carefully across the
lifting floor, her eyes on Deidre all the while before looking
down at her watch as she sat beside Mabombo. "Ah," she
said with a smile, "still early, so I can say good morning. I
hope you are well, Miss van Deventer."

"No, I'm not well. I'm tired of this fucking bullshit. I want to go home. I don't have anything to say to you people."

Xaba placed the bags on the table. "Please, Miss van Deventer, we only have a few more questions. I see you have a nice cup of tea there. We can wait a minute for you to enjoy that before we continue. It won't take long."

"Just ask your questions and hurry up." But she picked up the mug, drank from it, drank again. "So, what else do you have?"

Xaba held out one of the bags she had brought in with her. "Do you recognize this?"

Deidre spread out the plastic, peered closely. It was something cloth-like, covered in dirt.

"I don't even know what it is."

"And this?" She held out another bag.

"No."

"Please, look at it."

"For fuck's sake, I am looking. What do you want me to say? Is it a T-shirt? That could have belonged to anyone."

"No, not to anyone, Miss van Deventer. Please, take a closer look." She had been holding the bag out, but she leaned over toward Deidre now, put it on the table, pointed to the inside of the neckline. "Can you read that?"

Deidre bent forward, squinting. "I don't know, my eyes are—" She read the words. Sat back. Crossed her arms.

"Can you tell me what it says, Miss van Deventer?"

"You know what it says."

"Please, what does it say?"

"It's my name."

"That's correct. Can you tell me why your name is on the inside of this T-shirt? A T-shirt that we found wrapped around the body of a dead baby?"

"I had nothing to do with that!"

"Whose handwriting is it?"

"Listen, you have to—"

"Whose handwriting is it?"

"My dad's, but—"

"So your father wrote this?"

"It was from when I was in hospital. He put my name on all my clothes with a pen, like a permanent marker for clothing, to prevent stealing and stuff. That's all. He had nothing, I'm telling you, nothing to do with killing anyone. He just wasn't that kind of person. There's no way."

Xaba held out another bag to her. "And what about this one? Do you recognize it?"

Deidre leaned with her elbows on the table, her fingers pressing into her brows.

"Miss van Deventer, I am asking whether you recognize this?"

"Yes."

"What is it?"

"A handkerchief."

"Whose handkerchief?"

"Ross's."

"And how do you know that?"

She gestured at the bag. "Why are you asking me this? For fuck's sake, you can see for yourself, those are his initials." Then, quieter, "My mom made a bunch of them when he was young. We all had them."

"And did he ever use them?"

"I don't know. How can I know? Where did you find it?"

Xaba turned to Mabombo, whispered something, turned back. "It was found stuffed into the mouth of one of the babies. It is possible that it was put there to stop the baby from crying."

Deidre put a hand to her lips, biting down hard on her forefinger. "No." She closed her eyes, her chin trembling. "No."

"I'm afraid it's true."

"No. You've made a mistake. You're wrong. My dad found a skeleton of a dog. I told you about that other family. There was a skeleton of a dog. That's what you found. It's not a baby. I'm telling you."

Xaba picked up a pale green folder from the table, took out several pages on which color photographs had been printed, two to a page. She handed them across. Deidre wiped her hand on her skirt, took them. She could see soil, and things in the soil; the T-shirt, other bits of fabric. But then the soil seemed to fall away and they began to peer out at her, with large eyeless sockets. Little skulls. Little human skulls, surrounded by fabric and earth. She didn't look beyond the first two pages, handed them back to Xaba. "I don't understand. What was the point of killing them?"

"That's what we are trying to find out." She returned the photos to the folder. Then, "I need to ask you about the terrorist group that your brother joined in, we think, the end of 1993 or early 1994."

"Stop calling them that. They weren't fucking terrorists. They were just . . . I don't know."

"They had your brother making bombs for them. They had a stockpile of weapons and plans for upsetting the country's first free and democratic election process. You don't consider that a terrorist action?"

"Look, I told you people this before, back when it happened. None of us knew anything about the men or the bombs or any of their plans. Ross and I weren't close. I knew nothing about him."

"The men in the group were all in their forties and fifties, some even older. Where would Ross have met these people?"

"I've said all of this before. I have no idea. He went off on a Saturday to the hardware store a lot of the time or sometimes on a Friday night he'd say he was going to meet a friend. My mom would sometimes drop him off, but he always got a lift back. I don't know where he'd been. I just thought he was going to someone's house."

"Did you ever see him with any of these older men?"

"I never saw Ross with anyone. Ever."

"So, you never saw them?"

"No, only when their photos were published in the paper afterward. That's the first I ever heard of them or saw them. I was in the hospital. Nobody spoke about them."

Xaba made a note, put down her pen, folded her hands in front of her. "We have been able to speak to one of the five men; he's the only one still alive. But he has dementia."

"And? What does he say about the babies?"

"It's hard to know what he knows . . . But, Miss van Deventer, the fact is that he and the others were in jail already by the time we suspect the babies were killed."

"Okay, they were in jail, but Ross wasn't around either, remember. He'd run away. He wasn't here."

"Traces of newspaper were found around one of the corpses; it had been partially protected by the T-shirt, so we have been able to determine a date: seventh of July 1995."

"You see, he wasn't here then, so it couldn't have been him."

"Is it possible that he returned home? Do you remember seeing him?"

"No, of course not. Never."

"Are you sure you never saw him or had any indication that he had been there?"

"No, I mean, he phoned a few times, but—"

"He phoned? You spoke to him?"

"No, not me. I mean, I'm not even sure if he phoned, we just sort of guessed, me and my dad, because of how my mom behaved."

"How was that?"

"I don't know."

"Miss van Deventer, please, this is very important."

"It only happened a few times . . ."

"What happened?"

"She'd go into some kind of weird state. Like she'd clean his room, bake a ton of biscuits for him, send my dad out to buy clothes for him. And she'd lay the table with food and biscuits that none of us were allowed to touch. But he never came. So, when six, seven days had passed and he hadn't come, we would throw away the food, and chuck the biscuits out into the garden for the birds. After the second time, my dad, he was the one that guessed maybe Ross had phoned to say, I don't know, that he was coming back maybe. But it could just as easily have been my mom losing her mind."

"Is it possible that he did visit at those times?"

Deidre put her head on the table. She closed her eyes, saw darkness, and within it were two arcs of some greater darkness, something that thinned and grew, thinned and grew, a pulse that settled in her throat, in her bladder.

"Miss van Deventer?"

She lifted her head, felt the plastic tablecloth peel away from her cheek.

"I am asking you, could he have visited? Is it possible?"

"I don't know. I don't fucking know. I mean, what am I supposed to say? You tell me my brother was a terrorist, that he kidnapped and killed babies. What can I say about it? What the fuck can I say about it?"

Xaba waited. Then, "We want to hear anything you have to tell us."

She shook her head. "No. There's nothing I can say."

He drove her back along roads too quiet for the middle of the day. The mountain continued to burn, the smell of it filling the air, making their breath heavy and foul. She could hear the helicopters, but not see them. Mabombo put the radio on again, letting her sit in her silence and look out of the window, hands tight on the strap of her bag. Tears threatened, and she clenched her teeth. "I don't want this," she said. "I don't want this."

They passed streets and blocks she had known all her life, yet everything had altered, was deserted, ash covered. They stopped at a traffic light. She looked out at a brief row of shops to her right. At one time there had been a post office, a dentist, but both had long since closed, the dentist retiring, the South African Post Office bankrupt. There was a faded To Let sign in each of the shop windows. Beside them, an Animal Welfare charity shop, its door closed, but an Open sign hanging on the glass panel. Hard to see inside, see if anyone was moving beyond the shoes and photo frames and paintings and clocks on display in the front window. One shop over was the liquor store, its door open. She knew the place well enough, knew it wasn't likely to close because of a fire. And, as though to prove her point, the owner himself came to the entrance, squinting out into the soot, looking up and down the street. She hadn't seen him since the move to Oak Bend and felt an urge to roll down the window, shout hello. He'd been a friend to her, in his way.

But she looked instead toward the traffic light as it changed to green. They moved forward along the main road, going slowly, Mabombo leaning forward, concentrating on what lay beyond the blur. Blocks later and she could still see the owner of the shop, Essley was his name, standing there in front of her. Essley whom she'd visited once a week, then two or three times, then daily. Essley with his cheap cologne and ironed T-shirts amidst the smell of greasy samosas staling at the counter. Metal shelves lined the walls, filling the floor space, every part of them covered with bottles. She could walk in there this minute, a scarf over her eyes, and find whatever she wanted. Whiskey, brandy, rum, vodka, the cheap tetrapaks of red and white wine; knowing them by feel and habit.

She had been there when they called her. A surprise, the phone ringing like that in her pocket, making her jump a little, laugh at herself. It was her first cellphone, still new, barely used beyond a call from Monica on the house's landline, while she stood in the other room and waited to pick up and say, "It's working."

She'd answered, spoken too loudly, and left, buying nothing. Easier back then to go without a drink for a day. She'd stood outside, closed her eyes, lowered her head. That phone call, telling her that they had what they believed might be Ross's body, and would she mind coming in to identify him, any time that was convenient, but sooner rather than later, please, if she would be so kind.

She'd had to take a minibus taxi there, all the way to the old morgue, out in Salt River it was then, and no offer to reimburse her for it. They'd made her wait. An hour, ninety minutes, on a plastic garden chair until someone could come and meet her, even though she'd told them she was coming right in and they should have been expecting her. Later, being led along gray-painted floors into a flickering luminescence, where three metal trolleys were lined up side by side, each of them covered with a sheet. A man pointed at the left one, waited for her to join him beside it. She had approached, thinking it further than it was, so that she bumped into the edge with a crutch, set the trolley in motion, made it move away just a little. The man steadied it, said, "Oops." He pushed the trolley back into place and she looked down at the wheeled foot, where bits of hair and mop strands had caught and gathered.

"Are you ready?" he said, taking hold of the end of the sheet, the hem loose, several frayed holes visible.

She nodded and watched as he pulled it back to reveal head and neck, nothing more.

She saw the beard first, the size and color of it. Unkempt, already a few white hairs at the edges, making him seem so old, though he would have been young still, not much over thirty. The bottom lip was chapped, the top hidden under a long mustache. His hair, too, was long, wiry, with streaks of gray. Blackheads pitted a large nose and spread out across his cheeks. Just above his right eyebrow was a flesh-colored mole that she did not remember and a few acne scars on his cheeks that she didn't remember either. Below his ear she could make out the lines of a tattoo and she pointed. "Can I see this?"

"Of course." He came forward, pulled back the sheet to just past the shoulder, then held the beard to one side, revealing a naked woman, a cartoon, posing in such a way that you could see her breasts, her bum. It was badly done, probably a home job.

"Do you know where they found the body?"

"Ja, we've had a few in from the same place over the years. It's this abandoned building out in Woodstock where some people live."

"You mean like a drug house?"

"Something like that."

"And that's how he died? From drugs?"

"Yes."

The man was gaunt, seemed to have been hungry for a

while. There had been stories about that in the tabloids. About white people losing their jobs, not being able to find any others, of losing everything and having to live on the streets, where they were starving to death. There were photos of white children begging, of white women working as domestics for black families. A world on its head. A world that had been feared by some and that was easy to point at now, these few cases, and to say, "You see, you see."

She looked down at the man again, his beard and nose, that cheap tattoo, searching for something, some mark or sign, putting her hand out as though that action were enough to grasp hold of it. But the skin was cold, and she drew away.

"I don't know this man," she said.

"You're sure?"

She shook her head. "How can I be?"

Already there was too much noise as she entered. The bar full, the tables occupied. She held back, the early morning's sickness with her again, and a fever starting to grow. Still in her mind were the ziplock bags, the artifacts and obscurities that had been exhibited, paraded, pushed under her nose, and now the memory, too, of the dead stranger.

It was always this way with Ross. He took over all things. It was his memory, his hobbies, his behavior. He was the one they spoke of. He the one they returned to again and again, throughout her life. Even when he had left, even when it should have been about her, there he was. In the interrogation room, in the morgue, the hospital bed, in the house among the cracks and dirt, and here too, even here he made himself felt. Moments before, as she stepped out of the car, Mabombo had opened the door for her, held out the crutches. "Ma'am, all of this about your brother must be very hard for you. I want you to know, you have my number, and I want you to know, please, that you can call me, even just to talk."

She'd laughed then, took the crutches and shook her head as she stepped onto the pavement. "Really? That's what you want me to know?"

Mabombo had his hand on the door, looked at her, looked away. "I just—I don't think you should be alone with all of this about your brother."

"You don't think I should be alone with it?" she'd said. "Nice for you, isn't it? Really nice for you when you're the one who brought it to me. It's you that did this, you brought it to me and made me be alone with it. Don't come with this bullshit now about phone calls. I told you, I don't want any part of this."

She had walked toward the entrance, had not turned back when he said something behind her, yet she stood now in the open doorway, reluctant to enter.

But then she saw Isaac behind the bar, knew him, was able to claw her way back into certainty. She pushed through the noise toward him, had to shout before he saw her and came over.

"Hey, man," she said, "what's going on here?"

"Ag, you know, it always gets like this when there's a fire. People want to get drunk when the world is going up in flames around them."

"Ja, I know the feeling. I could fucking well do with a drink."

He leaned closer. "Listen, go find Marvin. He's won

some money on the horses and he's been buying rounds for people."

"Really?" She turned, looked back into the room, couldn't see him at once, then found him near the passage, coming toward the bar. She called to him from where she stood, "Hey, Marvin. I hear I have to congratulate you. How much you win anyway?"

"A shitload, a fucking shitload."

"Ja, really? After all these years, you finally one of the big boys, hey?"

"That's right, that's absolutely right. Today is my fucking day. It had to come eventually, hey?"

He stumbled toward her, his movements jerky, a shirt button undone so that his belly showed. There was sweat on his forehead, his hair wet with it, and more in patches under his arms and across his chest. He laughed as he reached her, his breath smelling strongly of booze, of cheese-and-onion chips.

She turned her head a little, breathed through her mouth. "Well, Big Boy, aren't you going to buy me a drink so I can celebrate with you?"

He put his arm around her, his shirt damp on her skin. "Of course, baby, of course. Anything for the most beautiful woman in the room." He turned to Isaac. "Please, signor, a shot for the lady, and one for me."

Isaac poured out Jägermeister for each of them. Marvin handed her the shot glass. "To winning!"

"To winning," she replied, the liquid spilling a little as

they toasted. She swallowed it in one, returned the glass to the counter, began to lick her fingers. "That was nice," she said, "but how about the Big Boy gets me something a little stronger this time?"

"Anything you want, baby, anything."

"Double Red Heart," she said to Isaac.

He poured and she drank it down.

"I got to go pee," Marvin said, already fumbling with his zip as he staggered toward the toilet.

"Jesus," she said under her breath, then to Isaac, "Right, I want two more doubles, but make one with Coke."

"Who's paying for it?"

"He can." She nodded at Marvin's back.

"No man, Deidre, you know I can't do that. Not without him telling me."

"Oh, for fuck's sake. I'll pay for it then. I've got money. Look, I've got money." She took her card out of her purse, waved it in his face.

He poured again, got a can of Coke and pulled the tab for her, then brought across the machine. By the time she'd tapped, she'd knocked back one of the glasses and was pouring Coke into the other.

She returned the card to her bag, looked for a place to sit. There was an empty table in a corner on the other side of the room. She patted the shoulder of the man next to her, said, "Hey, do me a favor and take my drink over there."

He turned in surprise, seemed about to say something,

but then looked her up and down, saw the stump and crutches. He slid off the stool, said "Sure, of course" to her and "Don't drink my beer" to his friend.

He was young, not even thirty yet, and tall, easily a head above everybody else. She followed him to the table, letting him pull out the chair for her and lean the crutches against the wall.

"Everything okay?" he said. "You need anything else?"

She was feeling warm now, good. She smiled up at him, put her hand out. "Ja, why don't you come sit with me a bit?"

But he drew back, shook his head. "Oh, sorry, I can't. I'm with a friend. Thanks."

He returned to the bar, and she mouthed "Gay" after him while she put her hands to her hair, pushing it around so that it looked tousled, then adjusted her top so that her cleavage showed. She drank, looked around, but everyone had their backs to her, looking elsewhere.

Then from close by, "Hey, hey, what's going on here?"

"Well, look who it is."

Trevor came to stand beside her. "How you, Deidre?"

"How am I? Jesus, man, look at you!" His hands and face were black with soot, a strong smell of woodsmoke on his clothes. "What happened?"

"I know, I know. I've been up at Cecilia Forest helping with the fire."

"Always the Good Samaritan, huh?"

"I do my bit."

"Well, how about doing another bit and coming to sit with me."

He looked at his watch. "Okay, but it can only be quick, hey. I'm really tired. I just came to have a beer and then I was planning to go straight to bed. I have an early shift again tomorrow and I'm exhausted, man, just exhausted. What you drinking? Can I get you anything?"

"Ja, Red Heart and Coke. Double."

She dug in her purse for lipstick but found only lip balm. She applied it, rubbed her lips together with difficulty. They were numb, her tongue too, her whole face numb. She put her hands to her cheeks, felt nothing. She remembered the dead man again, and her brother, the man's face on her brother's teenage body. Shook her head, made herself laugh, about nothing, only to laugh and forget the dead.

Trevor returned, put drinks on the table. "Geez, it's chaos in here today."

She took her hands from her face, felt herself speaking. "Ja. Like Doomsday, that's what my mom always said if we went to town on a Saturday morning and there were too many people and nowhere to park, she'd say, 'It's like Doomsday here!'"

"Ja, my mom was the same." He took a sip of his beer. "It does sort of feel like the end of the world though, when you're up there on the slopes. I mean, this fire, it's bad.

Really bad. They say there's already houses burning all across the peninsula, like wherever you look. It feels hopeless, almost like what's the point."

"So, don't go back tomorrow."

He shook his head. "That's not the way it works."

"Then do what you want, what do you want me to say?"

He blinked. "What's wrong? You having another bad day?"

She picked up her glass, drank.

"You have to learn to look for the good in things, Deidre. I know lots of people who are in terrible situations, but they manage to turn it around. I see it all the time at that charity I told you about. People really trying hard when they have nothing, and they do it with smiles on their faces. There's always something we can do to—"

"Please, I'm not in the mood for this charity stuff right now. You do your charity, you rescue all of us from being burnt alive, okay, so you're amazing, you're a goddamn hero, but leave me out of it, okay?"

"No, it's not like that. I'm just saying that all of us can help each other and—"

"Why would I help anyone else? I'm the one that needs help," she said, poking her chest with a finger. "Me. Look at me. I'm the one!"

"What do you mean?"

"What do I mean?" Her head hung a bit as she spoke, and she had to look up at him, her shoulders feeling like they could collapse and thrust her forward onto the table at any moment. "I mean that I was eighteen years old. Eighteen and I lost everything. What did I have after that? What could I become, huh? Everything was taken from me. Everything. That's what this country took from me. My whole fucking life, and gave me nothing in return. Not a fucking thing." She gave a sob, brought the glass to her lips.

Trevor put his hand out and touched hers. "Hey, maybe that's enough for today. Come on, why don't I take you home?"

Her head lolled, the table close now, very close. She looked at his hand on hers, said, "Oh, it's like that, is it?" Then leaned over clumsily, putting her hand directly on his groin. "Come on, darling, let's go. I'm ready."

He took her hand, returned it to the table. "Don't do this, Deidre."

She gave a hoot, tried to clap, her hands missing one another. "Oh Jesus, you're afraid! You're afraid I'll find out about your limp little charity dick. That's what it is, hey?"

He rose, picked up her crutches, held them out to her. "Come on, let me take you home."

She took them from him, stood with difficulty. He tried to help her, put his arm out to steady her. She jerked away. "Get your fucking charity dick hands off me."

"Deidre . . ."

She moved back toward the bar, saw Marvin standing there among the other customers, and called across to him, "Hey, Marvin! Marvin, come here."

He waved, stumbled over. "Hello, beautiful."

She took hold of his arm, pulling him nearer. "We're celebrating, right? You and me, we're celebrating."

He nodded, held up his glass. "That's right, of course it's right. We celebrating."

Trevor looked at her. "Last chance, Deidre. Let me give you a lift home. You're not in good shape."

"Not in good shape?" She pulled on her top, brought it down to reveal her bra, her pushed-up breasts. "You don't think this is good shape?"

Marvin laughed. "It looks really good to me," he said, and she turned with him toward the bar.

There was banging on a door, a voice shouting, "Come on, we're closing. I'm going to lock you in."

Her stump rested on a basin, beside it a filthy toilet, a urine-soaked floor. Her underwear had been pulled to the side, was cutting into her thigh and backside. And on her neck the cheese-and-onion chips smell of Marvin's breath as he pushed in and out of her.

The neighborhood was dark as she crutched back along the quiet road, no light since the night's loadshedding began, and nothing to be expected until 5:00 A.M. Always the same, this pitching into fumbling black. But there was the fire, the glow of the burning mountain, stretched long across the horizon, guiding her back to where she lived. And no pain now. Everything that had been angry and violent was at sleep.

Yet soon there came a confusion of lights, and she stood still, brought a forearm up to her eyes. A car approaching, its music loud, the bass so low that her crutches vibrated against her. The driver was hooting, his passengers laughing, hanging out the window as they passed, banging on the side of the car, calling out to her, cheering and yelling, and she raised her arm away from her face, waved at them, filled all at once with joy at this unexpected companionship in the dark.

"How much, lady? How much?" they called, and she replied with something wordless, some whoop or howl that set them laughing again.

She could hear them minutes after they had driven on, could feel the bass still as she neared the complex. She continued to smile, whooped a few more times on her own, but quieting now, barely making a sound. The jolt had gone from her, and she felt only tired now, closed her eyes. Sleep came as she stood, but there was an interruption of light once more. A torch in her face. The nighttime security guard saying to her, "What's happened? Are you okay?"

She was hunched over, so tired that she could only lift the fingers of one hand from the crutch handle. "No, I'm fine."

He came closer, held the torch away from her face, but still she blinked at it. "Listen," he said, "are you hurt? Do you want me to help you, because I don't know about this. I mean, I really don't know about this. I don't know if I should let you in or not."

"No, I'm fine," she said again. "I'm going home now. There's wine next to my bed and I'm going home." She brought out her phone, searched for the torch function. "See, I'm fine. I'm fine. I've got my own light. I'll be fine."

But it was hard to walk with the crutches and the phone at the same time, so she paused a moment, put the phone in her mouth, took a couple of steps. That didn't work either, the phone already slipping from between her teeth. She began to bring it toward her top, so that she could hold it in place with her bra. But there was no top there, no bra. Nothing. Just her skin, her naked breasts. She tried to remember taking her clothes off, tried to think where they had been left, but she could remember nothing, not in this dark, walking toward sleep. She felt instead for her skirt, found it, and fit the phone into the waistband. Even so, she saw unclearly, bumped into walls, took wrong turnings before she was able to find her way to her corridor. And then the uncertainty, left or right, which number, which door was hers?

She looked in her bag for the keys, knocking the phone as she did. It fell to the floor, the torch going out. She tried to bend for it, could not balance, flopping for a while, unable to reach the ground. Then the phone's screen went dark, and the corridor was black. She felt a wall beside her, leaned against it, dropping the crutches as she slid onto the gritty carpet, and put her head back, burping rum.

It had been hours since she'd last thought of Ross; Ross with the dead man's face, Ross as he had been at the supper table when they were teenagers, drinking his Coke, giving his monosyllabic answers to their mother's questions. Here, in the lurching black of the corridor, he stepped out in front of her, as though he had been waiting all night for her to return. She put out her hand to him, could feel nothing. Nothing to be seen either. But she knew him to be there, knew he had come, could feel his breath, and she began to crawl, saying, "Wait for me. I can't see a thing."

"Hurry up. It gets narrower here, I can't turn around again."

She knew then where she was. Knew herself to have crawled away from the gritty carpet, out of the dark corridors of the old-age home, out of her broken body. Crawled so far away that she was thirteen years old in the mountain caves and tunnels above Kalk Bay. They had been allowed to take the train there during the school holidays, saying they were going to swim at the tidal pool at St. James. But they'd had no such plan, had a pamphlet in their backpack, under their towels and sunscreen and plastic-wrapped cheese sandwiches. Ross had found it—at the library, he'd said when he asked if she wanted to come with him. That had been a surprise, to be part of his secret.

The caves were dark, darker than she'd expected, and they had only one torch between them, a small one, smaller than a finger, that Ross had got in his Christmas cracker a fortnight before. He was the one who held it, swinging the weak beam about carelessly; the path unclear to her where she followed behind. From time to time he'd switch it off, stand still, and she wouldn't know where he was in the dark. He'd wait for her to panic, for her to call out, "That's not funny, stop it!"

But he'd let the darkness continue, hiding him. "Here, in this place where we are, right here, that's where they found bodies, thousands of years old."

"So what?"

"And do you know what was there, just under your feet?"

"Stop it."

"A skull, all smashed in. There wasn't a body, just the broken skull in a thousand little pieces."

"Ross."

She reached out to him, wanting him to stop, but managed only a gasp of sorts, surprised by what she felt. There was hair on his arm, and hard muscle beneath it. She did not remember those being there before. She withdrew her hand, said quietly, "I want to go."

But he would not move, said, "Wait, you haven't heard the best part. It was the skull of a baby!"

He switched the torch on, flashed it in her face. She brought her hands up, covered her eyes. She did not want to see him, did not want to see this stranger with his man's arms who had climbed out of the darkness. But the torch light was bright as daylight, and it came straight at her, eating into her hands, making its way through the gaps between her fingers, through her closed lids, coming for her eyes. She wiped the tears from them, began to see a face, a body, someone that had not been there before.

Then, "Jesus," she heard, "where are your clothes? Have you been here all night? You need to get up now, it's time to get up."

But she pulled away, would not be moved. "No, I have to go back."

Miriam reached down for her, took hold of her arms. "Get up, get up, you can't be here."

"I have to go back. I have to know where the baby came from."

Trudy

He came from the bathroom, carrying a small metal basin of warm water, a facecloth, and a bar of soap. The soap was old, half used up, had been left for some time to dry out, so that there were now deep cracks extending lengthways along its pink surface, and pale ridges beside them where layers had begun to peel away. He placed the basin on the bed next to her thighs, put the soap in the bowl, rubbed it between the palms of his hands until the water was cloudy and the soap smoother than it had been before. He lifted it out, moving toward the facecloth on the other side of the basin, allowing cloudy drops to fall on the sheet. He tried to build up a lather, but the cloth was still dry. He shook his head, put the soap on the sheet, dipped the cloth in the water, then wrung it out. He grabbed the soap, passed it over the cloth, getting a lather this time. Beneath his hands the sheet was a mess of suds and water. He saw her looking and said, "I'm sorry. I'll sort it out afterward."

He took her hand, his fingers cool and wet. Long fingers they were, thick and rough with years of work. She wondered what she might feel like to fingers such as those, with her doughy flesh, her forearms and hands dark-spotted, dry. He held her too firmly, scrubbed too hard, so that when she looked down at her arm, she could see faint pink swaths where he had passed the cloth.

He picked up her other hand, began again.

"You don't have to do that," she said. "The nurse takes care of all of this."

"No. I have to learn. There won't be a nurse when we're in the house. I have to know how to do this for you. I have to take care of you."

He wet the cloth once more, put soap on it, too much. She could feel the drops falling on the sheet across her stomach and hips, soaking through her clothes, making their way through to her skin, already cold. He said, "Shit," began to wipe at wet patches with the facecloth, spreading the damp, making it worse, her clothes sticking to her.

Pulling back the round neck of her nightdress, his eyes were fixed on the skin and bone of her collarbones, shy at the intimacy. He dabbed around the protrusions, dabbed at her neck, careful of the folds that hung there. He did not go behind her ears, went instead to her cheeks, stilling his breath as he wiped at the sleep gathered in the corners of her eyes. Lastly, as though he had been avoiding it, he made her lift her arms, exposing the flabby spaces where a few long hairs still grew. There were similar hairs on her chin, she knew. Sometimes Beauty or Pretty, or whatever the fat nurse was called, tried to pluck them out. But Trudy jerked her head at the pain, made it difficult. Now Pretty only trimmed them back, as she did with her fingernails and toe-nails, clutching Trudy's hand as though she were a new-born baby, whispering to her as she worked at the nails, milky and brittle.

He removed the bowl, didn't wash any other part of her. How like a son, she thought with a smile, to consider a mother as no more than a pair of arms and a pair of eyes, only ever someone reaching out to him, watching him. He came back with a towel, passing it over the wet patches beside her thighs, across her stomach. She winced at the pressure, shifted her legs. He looked up at her face, saw her pained expression, and said, "Oh, sorry." He lifted the sheet, exposing her wet clothes and skin, then draped the towel across her, pulling the sheet back into position, right up to her neck. She could still feel the cool dampness on her belly, but didn't say anything, didn't want to make him feel bad when he was trying so hard.

He went back into the bathroom. She could hear water splashing, a few notes sung low. When he came out he had washed himself, shaved off the stubble. He wore clean clothes; another pair of khaki pants and a different two-tone shirt, both showing the lines where they'd been folded. There was no smell of cigarettes on him, his breath fresh with toothpaste. He went to sit in the armchair, brushing back the wet strands of his hair with a plastic comb he had taken from the pocket of his shirt. He returned the comb, but didn't seem easy yet, letting his hands travel repeatedly to his head, pushing back the hair, making it smooth. At last he let them settle in his lap. Then he turned a little, so that he was facing the doorway, as though he were expecting someone.

"Who are you waiting for?" she said.

He looked up, nodded his head slightly. "Deidre."

PART FIVE

Deidre

She woke with the duvet pulled up to her neck, the mixing bowl beside her head. In her ears still Miriam's voice: "Jesus, Deidre, people could have seen you. Children could have seen you. And then what do I say to them, huh? How do I explain this?"

She sat up slowly, her mind already dark, her lungs thick, making her cough. There was the heat of fever, the hot discomfort of her cheeks as she held a hand to her face, still greasy with makeup and sweat. Something had lodged within her, and she coughed again to let it loose, though with each shudder the previous day's sickness pushed deeper into her, was sharp within her bladder and cunt. There seemed no other option now but to grab a knife, cut the pain out of herself, discard all that was rotten.

The coughing continued and she reached across to a mug on the bedside table, hoping Miriam had left water for her. But it was wine—poured by herself two nights ago and not finished before she had passed out. She brought it to her lips, drank slowly, let it loosen the inside of her mouth, release her teeth from her lips and cheeks. It was cool from standing out, cool still as it reached her throat, and she held the mug to her forehead, left it there a moment. There were chips along the rim, cracks from when it had fallen years before and she had glued it back together with a mess of yellow contact adhesive that had leaked and dried solid. It should have been thrown away, should never have been repaired, but she had wanted to keep it because it had been Monica's. She'd had a collection, displayed on shelves in her bedroom. They were arranged in a specific order, according to meaning or color or theme or whatever it was, and taken off the shelves once a week, dusted, placed back as before. She liked things to be just so, to remain just so. Always it was Monica who kept things tidy, who cleaned the house, who made sure everything was organized and in the right place. Even Trudy's room she had taken care of, though the old woman used to startle at the sight of her, looked at her each time as though she were a stranger. Yet it was she who had brought Monica to them, who had been seated on the couch in the lounge in the early morning with a baby in her arms.

Deidre rubbed a finger across the mug. MATRIC HIKE KNYSNA-WILDERNESS it read in flaking black text beneath a photo of a group of girls, so faded by now that she couldn't have guessed which was Monica, though she had known at one time. There were others like it in the kitchen cupboard, featuring school plays, friends' sixteenth birthday parties, the netball team, matric dance. But most of them had been given away when Monica packed up the contents of her room and said, "Take what you want, the rest is going to charity." She hadn't kept a single one for herself, not one to take with her when she left. "What for?" she'd said. "It'll just break." Though she could have used bubble wrap or rolled it in her clothes. But she'd shaken her head, said no.

Deidre drank the last of the wine, then leaned across to the bedside table, holding the mug under the spout of the wine box, turned the tap, the wine flowing slowly, almost finished now. She poured too much, the mug too full, spilling as she brought it unsteadily toward herself. It slopped onto the floor, the bedding, the bedside table, spreading toward a piece of paper that stuck out from beneath the box. She put down the mug, withdrew the paper. Monica's birth certificate, wet now. She wiped it on the duvet cover, wiped her fingers too, leaving smears behind. She hadn't asked Monica about it, had forgotten it was there. She looked for her phone, thinking she ought to send a message, ask if Monica needed it sent to her. But she remembered then what had happened, remembered it all at once, how she'd watched Monica turn out the contents of cupboard after cupboard, drawer after drawer, searching for this piece of paper. She had been preparing her documents so that she had everything she might ever need, everything so that she wouldn't have to return, and she'd been furious about it, saying, "I hate this place, this mess, the two of you just sitting here like you're already dead." She'd tossed her braids, slammed the door, taken a minibus taxi up to Home Affairs in Wynberg, where she was told it would be a six-week wait for a replacement, four if she was lucky. She'd had to postpone her flight, paying money she'd worked hard for, all of it wasted because Deidre had never taken the trouble to keep things in order. "Get yourself together, Mom," she'd said. "Please, you have to get yourself together. I'm not going to be here. You have to do it yourself." How many years ago now, those words? And here she was, the same. Exactly the same. Nothing changed. Nothing ever fucking changed.

She threw the duvet from her, stood up, the air cool on her fevered skin. She moaned at the pain within her, each movement a jolt, so that she stayed hunched over, unable to straighten up. Bent as she was, she could see her naked breasts, feel the shame of them, and she hunched further, wishing them forgotten, the entire night forgotten. She took the mixing bowl from the bed, dropped it on the floor in front of her, began to remove her panties. They were torn at the seams, smelling of semen, damp with it still, and she tossed them from her before squatting over the bowl with difficulty, the pain altering as she moved, so that it seemed wider now, seemed to be spreading throughout her abdomen, back into her anus, and she thought she might start shitting hot, dark blood. She waited for it to come, leaned her head against the side of the bed, waiting for all that was rotten within her to come rushing out. But nothing came. Only the sickness, the dreadful sickness that would not leave her, all of it still held fast within her. She reached up, took the full mug from the bedside table, drank furiously, letting it spill down the sides of her mouth, over her collarbones, over the shame of her breasts. Then allowed herself to lower her body, the weight of her causing the mixing bowl to slip out from under her, come up beside one of her thighs. She hung her head, gave in to the fever, let everything distort into sickness. She thought again of the knife, of taking it to her body. Thought of what it would be to be released from herself.

In the passage now the sound of Miriam and her boy. His voice pitched with excitement, telling a story about the school day in fits and starts. Her replies lower, slow, letting him get through it in his own way. Deidre roused herself, struggled up, pushing the mixing bowl under the bed. She took a T-shirt from the floor, put it on, waited for them to stop at her place, to pop their heads round her door and say, "Just checking how you are."

She would say she was sick, that she needed pills and water. Miriam could go buy some, just up at Hussain's would be fine, she didn't need to get in her car and drive to Checkers. Just up to Hussain's for a liter or two and a few paracetamol, that was all she needed. She stretched across to the headboard, where her bag had been left hanging, getting it ready on her lap so that she could wave her debit card in Miriam's face and say, "I'll pay for it, don't look at me like that. I'll pay for it, and you can even buy the boy a sweet if you like."

But they didn't stop, went straight on to their own room without a pause. She could hear them clearly in the late morning's quiet, hear the door being unlocked, the boy laughing, cupboards opening and closing, the TV coming on, and a short, sharp cry from Roxy.

She put the card back in her bag, put her hand inside, felt around for loose pills, couldn't feel anything, then turned it upside down, let the contents drop out onto the bed. The bank card, her ID, three bottle tops, a lighter, a heartburn tablet. She took the tablet, chewed it dully. Her phone had been in the bag too and she picked it up now. The screen had a large crack across the bottom that hadn't been there before, and the background picture had been changed. A group of men and women standing in what seemed to be the Nine Lives parking lot, with red cheeks and noses, none of them known to her apart from Marvin on the end with his stomach showing. She was in the middle, half naked, smiling at the camera. One of the women was pointing at her chest, a man had an arm around her shoulder, a hand on her breast. She swallowed, closed her eyes, put the phone back in her bag.

Her crutches were at the foot of the bed and she stretched for them, made her way to the kitchen, opened the cabinet above the sink. The carton of cigarettes was in there and she took it down, standing on tiptoe to check that none of the packs had fallen out and stayed behind. There were only four left, and she had no memory of having smoked the rest. She took one of the packs, returned the carton to the cabinet. Her hands shook as she peeled away the plastic, shaking more as she struggled to draw a cigarette out, eventually having to upend the packet on her palm. She picked one, let the rest slide back, put the cigarette to her lips. There was no smoking allowed inside the building, still she went back to the bed, looked through her bag for the lighter, and brought it up to the cigarette, sitting down to inhale and exhale, making sure to breathe toward the window, her back to the smoke sensor.

She was sick, that she knew. Needed water, needed pills. She'd have to go by herself, bad as she felt, she'd have to go. She took her bag again, slung it over her shoulder, sidestepped the panties on the floor, so that she came face-to-face with the mirror; a frameless thing, the size of a floor tile, glued to the wall outside the bathroom. She paused at the sight, saw herself frown. Sagging cheeks, clogged pores, balding eyebrows. Thin lips stained purple with wine. Yellow eyes and large, dark bags that spoke of age and sickness and mess. She looked away from herself, to the edge of the mirror, noticing what she had long since forgotten was there—a passport-size photo of Monica, taken at school in her matric year. She was smiling in the picture, her hair pulled back to reveal bright cheeks and forehead, her teeth as white as the collar of her shirt. The blazer had braiding around the edges to show academic excellence, and all the way down the lapels were badges for drama, choir, netball, Student Council, and one for her position as debating captain. And nothing in that young, smiling face that resembled her own, not as she was in the mirror today, not as she had ever been. Not like any of them at all. Nothing to link the two of them to one another but the years spent in that house, the years in that house as it prepared to fall down around them.

She remembered the cave, remembered the dark fear. "Where did it come from?" she heard herself say. "Where did the baby come from?"

She had to sign in, the nausea still with her, her head pounding as she opened her bag to let the security guard peer in and then wave her through the booms, telling her to report to reception. There she handed over her ID card, watched the number being written down, was asked whom she had come to see. Behind the receptionist a woman was returning a folder to a filing cabinet. She looked up at hearing "Trudy van Deventer" and came forward, her smile tightening as she took in Deidre's face and clothes. "Are you a relative of Mrs. van Deventer?"

"Daughter."

She came out from behind the counter, gave her hand. "Matron Fuzile. I'm glad you've come. Your mother receives very few visitors, only one, in fact. A friend of yours, I believe."

"Yes."

She looked her over again, said, "Well, why don't I show

you to your mother's room? I'm going that way myself."
She extended her arm, let Deidre go ahead of her down a
corridor to the right of the reception area.

The interior was almost identical to Oak Bend—the
same paint, the same bright prints against the walls, the
same blinds and curtains. But the rooms were even smaller
than her own; just space enough for a single bed and a chair,
and a small bathroom en suite. Each room had a door with
a glass pane in it, yet most of them stood wide open, showing old men and women lying in their beds, eyes fixed on
the ceiling or wall. A few stared out into the passage, their
lips trembling words they wished to speak to the people
passing by.

The carpet was in the same forlorn state as that at Oak
Bend. She had been walking slowly, but still her crutch
caught on a loose edge, made her stumble, made her stomach leap up and disgorge itself into her mouth. She swallowed back the mix of acid and wine, the rum and shots,
sick once more at the taste of it so that she couldn't keep it
down, could feel it begin to dribble past her lips, leak onto
her chin.

"Oh my God!" said the matron. Then calmer, "Are you
all right?"

Deidre nodded, heaved air, the acid rising again.

The matron grabbed a chair from the side of the passage, placed it beside Deidre. "Sit down," then reached into
her pocket, drawing out several crumpled tissues and
handed them across. Deidre took one, sat still, breathing

sharply until the matron said, "For goodness' sake, wipe your mouth."

She did, with a shaking hand, then balled the purple stains into her fist so that she didn't have to look at what had come from inside her. She was sweating now, her clothes sticking to her, her face hot. Yet her back felt cold, her chest too, and she began to shiver. She breathed out wetly through pursed lips, brought a hand to her throat.

"Are you going to be sick again? Do you need a basin?" said the matron.

"Uh-uh."

"I can see you are unwell." She'd folded her hands in front of her, was frowning up and down the corridor. "I think it's better if you come another day."

"No," she said, standing up slowly. "No, I'm fine. I need to see my mother."

The matron frowned again. "This way."

They went left into another corridor, continuing forward past more open doors until coming to a stop outside a room with her mother's name on a piece of paper within a perspex frame. The matron tapped on the door, looked in, spoke quietly, "Mrs. van Deventer?" then turned and said, "She's asleep, I'm afraid."

"I'll wait."

"Just so you know, there are nurses coming and going all the time. You are not to upset her—you will be asked to leave, you understand?"

She nodded. "I'm fine now. It'll be fine."

The matron gave Deidre a last look, began to speak, then shook her head and went back along the corridor.

Deidre entered the room. It was dim inside, the curtains and blinds drawn so that the only light came from the passage. She could see a bed, a chair on the other side of it, but not much else. Not beyond a shapeless form, lying without movement. She came around the foot of the bed, pulled back the curtains, turned the wand of the blinds so that the slats shifted slightly, allowing light to enter, brightening the room in narrow bands. The shape on the bed clarified itself into a version of her mother that she didn't remember. White hair, freshly brushed, hanging loose past her shoulders. A face she would not have known, so pleated and sunken had it become. The sheet was pulled up to her chin and, lying as she was, looking as she did, she seemed already dead.

Deidre put her head down, rubbed at her eyes and temples. She was hot still, hadn't been to Hussain's yet, had had no water, nothing for the pain and sickness. When she looked up, all was blurred and she fumbled toward the bedside table, opened the drawer, blinking several times before she could look inside and see there was no medication there. She glanced across at her mother's face, watched her eyelids flicker, but they did not open, and she continued sleeping with short breaths that lifted the sheet a little, lowered it again.

"Ma," Deidre whispered.

She'd only been home from the hospital for a week or

two, that final time, that very last time of all the many times, when she'd entered the lounge on that morning, her hands still blistered from the crutches that she hated, hated so fucking much, and she was going to the lounge so that she could sit on the couch and watch TV, meaning to stay there all day, have food and drink brought to her. But her mom was already there, sitting upright in her dressing gown, with the baby in her arms, her lips chewed to red. Deidre had called for her dad and they had sat beside her, the two of them, sat down and asked her where the baby had come from and she'd told them that Ross had been there in the night. She'd heard him tapping at the back door and she'd gone to open it. He embraced her and said he couldn't stay, but he'd brought the baby, his own little girl, for them to care for because raising a child wasn't possible when you were hiding from the authorities.

Her father had gone to an all-night pharmacy, bought formula and a bottle, newborn nappies, a gray onesie, coming home to feed her, change her. He took her out of the newspaper and T-shirt she'd been wrapped in, exchanged her old onesie for the new one, and folded her in a blanket he'd found at the top of the linen cupboard, left over from when Deidre had been little. The three of them sitting in the lounge throughout, none of them saying a word. Afterward they'd dressed, her father having to help each of them, so that when it was her mother's turn Deidre was left to hold the baby, staring down into its little black-edged eyes, humming songs she didn't know the words to. After

8:00 A.M. they took her to the private clinic near the racecourse, having to wait for a doctor who could see them
without an appointment, and when one was found, he
seemed harried, irritated at so many of them coming in together. He took the baby from them, began to undress it,
noticing the black knot of the umbilicus. "Whose child is
this?"

Trudy spoke first. "Our maid," she said. "Our maid had
the baby and then left it with us. She ran away."

He nodded, as though he had heard that often enough.
"Okay, I'll give you a number where you can report what
has happened. They'll tell you what to do. Was the mother
ill?"

Trudy shook her head. "I don't know."

"Well, we'll do a few blood tests anyway, check everything, and we'll check for HIV of course. A lot of mothers
with AIDS abandon their babies. It's a big problem, you
have no idea."

"And you'll test the rest?" her mother said. "You'll be
able to tell us what she is?"

He had hold of the baby's foot, was leaning down to in-
sert a syringe in the heel. "What do you mean?"

"You know," she wrung her hands, brought them up to
her mouth, "to tell us what she is, whether it's Xhosa or
Zulu or one of the others?"

The baby started to scream, her face crimsoning. He finished taking the sample, motioning to Deidre's dad. "You
can pick her up now." He placed the vial on a metal table

beside the cot and turned to her mother. "Ma'am, that's not . . . that's not something we can test for. There's no test for that, I assure you."

Her mother had lowered her head, said, "So we won't know?" and Deidre had looked down too, seeing the man's unpolished shoes, his black laces that had been tied twice over.

Her father gentled the baby's arms back into the onesie, secured the snaps, put the blanket around her again, hushing her softly.

The doctor glanced at them then, saw the baby screaming in her father's arms, saw his hunched shoulders, his furrowed brow, the pallor of her mother's cheeks, Deidre's bandaged stump. "Will you be keeping her?" he said, his voice loud in the small room.

Her mother began to speak, faltered, but her father said, "Of course," and later, when they were in private, "She's family, isn't she?"

Deidre stood up, grabbed hold of the side of the bed, shook her mother's arm through the sheet. "Wake up, Ma. Wake up!"

The eyes fluttered as they had done before, then opened slowly. She peered at Deidre, spoke in a whisper. "Is that you, my dear?" She looked around the room. "Where's Ross? Did you talk to him about the house?"

Deidre shook her head, kept hold of her mother's arm. "Forget the house, Ma. I need to know about Monica. You have to tell me, okay, you have to tell me where she came from."

Her mother shifted, bringing her hand unsteadily up from under the sheet, wiping hair from her forehead. "Water."

"What?"

She pointed to a plastic cup beside the bed. Deidre had not noticed it before, but picked it up now, held the straw to her mother's lips. She watched her sip with difficulty, saw her push the straw out with her tongue when she had done. Deidre brought the cup to her own mouth, drank down what remained, the water room temperature and tasting of plastic, then returned the empty cup to the bedside table.

"Ma, tell me."

"Why are you asking this? Where's Ross? What did he say to you?"

"He didn't say anything. I'm asking you. I came here to ask you. Where did Monica come from?"

"I told you, Ross came to the house, he brought her."

"But why did he have her? Where did she come from?"

She shook her head. "I don't remember."

"Don't lie to me," she said, her voice rising. "You're trying to lie to me. You said she was his daughter, that's what you said, remember? Is that the truth? Tell me."

"I don't know. He came to the house. It was the last time and he never came again after that."

"But he came before?"

She nodded, licked her dry lips. "A few times. He climbed over the back fence and I heard him. I wasn't sleeping, I couldn't sleep, I lay awake all night and I heard him when he came. I went to the kitchen and I saw him through the window, my boy coming home to me. I waited to let him in, but he didn't come to the door. He stayed down at the fence, with the hydrangeas. He went in underneath them and he didn't come out for a while, and when he did, he just left back over the fence."

"What else?"

"Nothing. There's nothing else."

"What else, Ma?"

"Nothing. He looked at the house before he left and I thought he had seen me, I thought he was telling me something, sending me a message."

"What kind of message?"

There were tears on her cheeks now, her lips trembling. "A message of love. To let me know he loved me. I waited to see if he was coming back, but when he didn't, I took the torch and I went down there and I crawled in where he'd been. The earth was loose and I dug a little, just with my hands, and I dug until I felt something and I thought that was it, that was the message."

"What was it?"

She shook her head.

"Tell me, Ma. You have to tell me. What did you find under the hydrangeas?"

She shook her head again, the tears running down into her mouth.

"Ma."

"It was a little face."

"And what did you do?"

"I covered it back up. I came inside. I washed my hands."

"You didn't do anything else? You didn't think to call the police or to tell anyone?"

"I did. I did tell someone. I told God. I went on my knees and said to Him, 'It's one life, just one life. Another mother's child so that mine can live. But just this once,' I said. 'Just this once.' Because Ross is special, that's the thing. He's special."

"Jesus, Ma. Jesus. Did Dad know?"

"No, never. No, he wouldn't have understood."

"Understood? What's there to understand? You let your son murder babies on your fucking doorstep, while you watched. He wasn't special. He was sick. There was something wrong with him. Can't you see that? It was murder, Ma, fucking murder."

"But I didn't know. I didn't know that."

"Of course you knew! How can you sit there and say you didn't know? He was killing them, you were killing them."

"No, not me. It wasn't me." She lifted her hands, brought them back down, clutching them in her lap. "And remember the last one, I saved her, that one I saved. You know I did. You know I saved her."

"But why?"

She paused a moment, closed her eyes, passed a hand over her mouth. "Because she cried. The others, they . . . But this one cried and I couldn't hear that, couldn't hear that crying and let him put a living thing into the ground. So I went outside and he looked at me and he seemed so frightened, no more than a child himself and so frightened, and he started to speak, but I said, 'No, my boy, that's enough now. That's enough.' And he let me take her from him and he said, 'Sorry, Ma,' and then he jumped over the fence and he didn't come back again, years and years and he didn't come back. And it was my fault because I chased him away. I chased away my boy and he never got to have the life he was meant to have. He never got to live as he should have."

"Oh Jesus. Oh Jesus. All this fucking time, Ma, all this time. We stole someone's baby. We stole a child and raised her in a fucking graveyard and you knew it the whole fucking time."

"I saved her."

"No, you didn't. Don't you understand that? Can't you see what you've done? How are we ever going to fix this? How can we ever hope to fix this fucking mess?"

She put a hand on Deidre's where it rested on the bed, said, "Don't worry, my dear. We'll speak to Ross, we'll ask him. He'll know what to do. We'll ask him and he'll know."

"Ma, stop saying that. Please, stop saying that."

Monica had already left when the phone call came. She was working as a barmaid in some village in the south of England, living in a hostel with Australians and New Zealanders, and sending messages about just hopping over to France quickly, or to Spain or Portugal, or going to Amsterdam and it was wild, Mom, so wild, you wouldn't believe it. She sent some photos too. Leaving Deidre to peer at the screen, looking at all the faces, closely, too closely, to see how they seemed—did they look like nice people? And then hating herself, thinking she was being just like her mother, exactly like she had been. But Monica seemed happy enough, with nice clothes, big warm jackets against the cold, gloves and beanies, things she'd never worn at home. And here she was, smiling like she'd only ever known snow and rain, like she spent her life stopping in the street to build a snowman on the pavement. It was as though she had been born to go away, to make a home for herself over there, far away from all of this shit.

The phone call came on the landline. Deidre answered from where she sat on the couch, still in her pajamas though it was the afternoon, watching kids' TV, one of the SABC channels. The woman said there was no doubt; they'd done fingerprints. It was him. He'd died in his sleep at a homeless shelter in Bloemfontein about eighteen months before, but it had taken this long to identify the body and contact next of kin, and, really, it had only been by chance, because normally these destitutes didn't end up being identified, so she was lucky. The woman said he'd already been buried some time before by the government, that the details would be sent to her and an exhumation could be arranged if they wished to bury him elsewhere.

"No, I don't want to know where he is," she'd said. "My mother is sick. She needs to believe he's alive."

But now she turned and said, "There is no Ross, Ma. He's dead. He died years ago. Your boy is gone, your child of the future is gone. There's only me. I'm what's left. It's just fucking me."

She walked through gutters that were dark with ash, residue sticking to the rubber feet of the crutches, powdering around the heel of her shoe. Black curls floated in the air. At the corner, two of the curls hung from the smooth surface of a stone bollard, both disintegrating as she went to sit upon it. The mountain was still on fire, though she could see no flames now, only smoke clouds. Even they were not what they had been, thinning out across the slopes above the winelands, showing through to smoldering swaths where the fire had done all it could.

Her mouth was dry, nausea and acid hard in her throat. She needed water. Had to have water. Everything about her burning and raw. She could feel the bones of her skull contracting with the heat of fever, could feel the tick-ticking of them becoming smaller, tightening until her head ached with the compression. She thought once more of knives, of bringing them to her body, cutting out that which was bad.

Began to imagine what she might look like afterward, something strangely formed, like that game she and her father had played with the dog skeleton years before. Only, there was so little that would remain of her after the cutting. A pair of eyes, a nose. Even they were too much, and she wondered if she might exist as thoughts alone, though those were dark with decay too, could not be allowed to stay.

She needed water, was desperate for it, but looked inside her bag instead, lit a cigarette. The smoke caught at the dryness in her throat, made her cough. She bent forward with the force of it, her tongue hanging out, lungs rattling with phlegm. Some of it came loose at last, jumped into her mouth, sat on the back of her tongue. She spat, but it wouldn't move, clinging there so that she had to work at it, coughing until the acid rose again and she retched it all out onto the pavement. A yellow clump bound by purple foam. Strands of saliva hung from her open mouth. They stretched out, broke, jumping back a little where they were still attached, her lips wet with them.

Across the way Miriam came out of the entrance to Oak Bend, pushing Roxy in a pram, the boy walking beside her. They paused a moment beside the security hut, spoke to Winston, and Deidre leaned on the crutches, pushed herself up. She began to call out to them, but she had moved too fast, was too unsteady. She fell forward, landed heavily, crutches beneath her, jolting her hip, her wrist, so that the call became a gasp.

But Miriam only glanced across, then turned to Winston

again, already shaking her head. He came out of the hut, looked at where Deidre lay, leaned in as Miriam whispered something to him. She was turning the pram, moving to face the other direction, toward the mountain. He walked a few steps with her, helped lift the front of the pram over the gutter, up onto the pavement while Miriam raised the back wheels and called to the boy where he stood staring at Deidre, told him to come to her at once. "We're going this way now," she said. When the pram was on the pavement, she reached across, put her hand on Winston's arm, spoke quietly again. He nodded and returned to his hut.

Deidre tried to sit up, to move her leg out from under the crutches. Her knee was grazed, blood already making its way down her shin. Her hands had been grazed too and she held them up, shook them as they stung, then reached inside her bag for the tissue the matron had given her earlier. She spread it out on her thigh, saw the purple marks upon it, remembering then what she had inside her, remembering what she had spat up moments before. She looked around for it, couldn't find it on the ground nearby, looked on her arms, her leg, until she found it smeared along the side of her shoe. She took the tissue to her knee first, wiped up the blood, then she brought her foot closer, wiped at the purple and yellow until the tissue was saturated.

She held it in her hand, made a fist, feeling the burn of the graze, the sodden contents, all that was rotten within her, all of that in her hand, damp and vile. She lifted her arm, tried to throw it away. But it stuck there, held fast by the weeping graze, and she had to open her hand, pick at the tissue with the fingers of her other hand, peel it off slowly.

The bollard was behind her and she shuffled toward it, pulled herself up, then took hold of the crutches, firm in each hand, pressing down with stinging palms until she was standing upright. She moved slowly, her knee and hip pain-ing, walked out, away from the gutter, into the side street, coming to a halt on the vertical white line of the stop sign and looked across toward the building where she lived, her room with its filth and memories, Monica looking out at her from the mirror's edge.

She took her phone out of her bag, went to her missed calls, pressed on the most recent, listened as it rang.

"Miss van Deventer?"

"I can't talk long, I don't have a lot of airtime."

"I can call you back."

"No," she said. "No, this'll be quick. I just wanted to ask you, what's going to happen now? I mean, with all that stuff you told me, what's going to happen?" Her voice wavered at the end and she took a moment to clear her throat.

Mabombo waited for her to finish. "Well, I'm afraid there isn't really very much we can do. There can't be a trial because to have a trial after the guilty party is dead, it's very rare. I mean, it just doesn't happen."

"So what was all of this even for? Why do this to me?"

"Miss van Deventer, this is difficult for you, of course,

but you must agree that the truth has to come out. To leave the thing alone would have been to deny it and cover it up. And we must consider the other people involved. Families lost their children, and have been living with questions and pain for all these years."

"But how will you even find them? I mean, how will you even know where to look?"

"We're looking into missing children cases, asking people to come forward. There are procedures in place for something like this."

"And you think it's fair?"

"What?"

"To do that after all this time, to bring up the past like that? Don't people just want to be left in peace to live their fucking lives? I mean, how does any of this make it better? This can't be better."

"Well, think of it this way, if it was your daughter who went missing thirty years ago, wouldn't you want to know what had happened to her? Wouldn't you be hoping every day for all those years to know if she was dead or alive?"

She didn't say anything, stood with the phone at her ear, looking down at her other hand, its open palm. The graze was dark where dirt remained, yet she could still feel the damp weight of the balled-up tissue in her hand, the color of it, the smell.

"Miss van Deventer, are you there? Shall I call you back?"

"No. No, I need to . . . Can you come here? Can you

pick me up? I'm here, I'm outside, in my street. I need to talk to you, I need to tell you something."

"Oh," he said. "Yes, I'll be there in a few minutes, just stay there and I'll be there soon."

She hung up the phone, returned it to her bag, then looked up at the burning mountain, the scarred face of it, slopes of black and ruin, the great smoldering expanse parched and heaving. If only the rain would come, just a little bit of rain, to wet the soil, feed the seeds, so that something might grow again.

ABOUT THE AUTHOR

KAREN JENNINGS is a South African writer based in Cape Town. Her novel *An Island* was longlisted for the Booker Prize. She is a writer in residence with the Laboratory for the Economics of Africa's Past (LEAP) at the University of Stellenbosch.